the last
to know

Claire Highton-Stevenson

DEDICATION

To all the friends who have beaten the odds and found their love together.

ACKNOWLEDGEMENTS

My editing team, who are constantly evolving me as a writer. Encouraging growth and expansion of my work with a gentle guiding hand.

CLAIRE HIGHTON-STEVENSON

PROLOGUE

June 2025

The church bells rang out as Caz Madden stepped out of the car and was greeted by her nearest and dearest, all dressed in their summery finery, as is the case for a June wedding in the southern counties of England.

It was obvious which side were her guests and which were Grace's. The queerness shone through in every direction she looked. Her mates from the bar, all in suits, fresh cuts, and a haze of aftershave, and those were just the girls.

Grace's side were much like Grace, more elegant and traditional. Men in suits, women in dresses and hats, all huddled together or around Grace's mum, Lila. Caz waved at them.

Dani, Caz's work bestie, called out and Caz grinned at her. Making her way over, Caz felt a little out of place in the dress, but they'd agreed they'd both only be doing this the once, and wasn't it every little girl's dream?

Even her hair was down, which didn't happen often, but she wanted Grace to be happy.

Caz was more of a tomboy than a girl's girl. Her comfort zone was jeans and shirts, hair tied up, getting her hands dirty—usually under a car.

Not today, though.

Her hair, dark and wavy, hung loose and framed her elfin face. She'd even let Grace's friend, Beth, do her make-up, though she insisted on keeping it light, no matter how much Beth tried to convince her she'd look like a film star with something more dramatic.

There were limits.

But Grace Hart meant the world to Caz, and if all she needed to do to make this day perfect for her was to put on a figure-hugging, floor-length, white gown, then who was she to say no. She did balk at the idea of heels, she was already three inches taller than Grace. Nobody would know she was wearing Converse All Star high-tops beneath it, but at least she knew she wouldn't trip and break her ankle...or her neck.

She'd gotten her own way for the reception at least, when they would both change into perfectly fitted suits and comfortable brogues. An agreement where Grace had said, *"It works well for the worlds we both live in now."*

They were already a team, weren't they? Always compromising, never arguing.

"You scrubbed up alright," Dani said when she reached the group. "I almost fancy ya myself." She laughed and jumped back at the playful thump she received.

"Thought I'd make the effort, you know, seeing as it is my wedding day and all that."

Dani rolled her eyes. "You still sure you wanna go through with it?"

"Yeah, course. Why wouldn't I?" she said, pushing away any remaining doubts as quickly as she'd swat a fly.

The eye roll gave way to a raised brow. "People don't marry people they've been mates with for years, out of the blue."

"Alright, I know that it's...different, and people didn't expect it, but I don't care. I love her. And she loves me, and that's all that matters."

"Okay, well, on your head be it." Dani tutted. "Getting married and leaving us."

The others nodded and patted her on the back like she were a doomed prisoner.

"I'm not leaving...we're still gonna be friends."

"Yeah, yeah, they all say that 'til—" She poked Caz in the ribs. "Heads up, she's here. We'd best get inside." Dani dragged Caz by the arm. "It's bad luck to see the bride."

"I am a bride."

"Exactly, double trouble, now move it."

Caz let herself be dragged towards the church alongside all the other guests filing in, but not before she took one last look over her shoulder.

The car with Grace inside had pulled up right between the entrance gates. Her dad had climbed out and was holding the door open for Grace, and that was all she was going to get to see.

"Excuse me, bride coming through!" Dani shouted. They made their way into the church and stood off to the side, waiting as guests passed by, smiling and offering wishes of good luck, and how beautiful did Caz look.

Caz took it all in her stride, trying not to let it all overwhelm her.

They'd agreed they wouldn't have bridesmaids or a best man. Dani got the job of walking Caz down the aisle.

"Right, catch ya breath. Let them all get seated, and then —" Dani wiped a bit of dirt from Caz's face. "Honestly, can't take you anywhere. You cleaned your nails, right?"

Caz held her hands up. "I'm not completely grim."

"You bloody are when you get under those cars."

The organ piped up, and all further conversation was done. "Let's do this," Caz said, linking arms with Dani. She glanced around at what should be her family's side of the church. It was filled with friends—no family. She didn't think it would bother her, and she was right—it didn't.

Growing up in care had meant she'd gotten used to family being people you chose, not people you were lumbered with by blood. And she had Grace and Grace's family, didn't she? She grinned. That was all she needed. All she'd ever needed.

"You alright?" Dani asked, noticing Caz drift off somewhere other than right there.

"Yeah, just thinking about family, and how mine is the one I created." She grinned again. "The future's so bright..."

"Gotta wear shades!" Dani joined in.

Graceful Grace—that was what they all said whenever she did anything, dance classes, gymnastics, yoga. Today would be no exception when she stepped out of the Rolls, made her way up to the church, and swept her way down the aisle.

Her white dress had been stitched to fit at great expense, but it was worth it. This one day in her life, she'd get to live out the fantasy of being a real-life princess.

And yeah, it might be a little unexpected to those who knew her, that it wouldn't be a *Prince* Charming standing at the alter waiting, but for Grace, it was someone much better.

Her best friend.

Caz was her person. Through thick and thin, they'd been there for each other.

It didn't seem crazy to them at all.

"Are you ready, Sweetpea?" her dad asked, using a nickname he'd used since she was old enough to remember. She was probably a bit old for it now, but still, it was comforting and helped settle the nerves.

She'd stopped to take a breath and look up at the blue sky, clear of clouds and warm from the sun. It was just the perfect day to get married and turn her life into the one she wanted to live—one with Caroline Madden.

"I am." She smiled and took the hand he held out for her. Tucking her arm through his, they listened to the bells for a moment.

"It's not too late to back out," he said quietly as they began to walk.

She turned to him, all smart in his navy suit, hair combed. "I don't want to, Dad. I know Caz will be the perfect partner."

He nodded. "We like Caz, you know that. I'm just saying, whatever you choose today, it doesn't change anything for us."

"I know." She frowned for a second. *Why couldn't everyone just be happy for them?*

Before she had the chance to dwell on that thought, they were there at the steps. The bells stopped ringing and the organ began to play for the second time.

"I just want to be Mrs Madden-Hart." She smiled confidently, and although they hadn't actually agreed on a double-barrelled name option, she thought it had a nice ring to it.

"Alright, then." He beamed. "Gotta admit, I didn't think I'd see the day when I walked my little girl down the aisle—thought we'd missed that boat."

"So did I," she grinned, "but here I am, and yeah, I know it's not what everyone expected, but—"

"Honestly, I don't think anyone could deny you and Caz are special together."

"Do you really think so?" she asked him as he adjusted her

veil.

"Yeah, the way you both look at each other when you think nobody else is looking? We've all seen it, but you had to find your way there by yourselves."

Grace smiled. *Had they been like that the entire time, without noticing themselves?*

They'd reached the part of the church where all she had to do was to turn, step through the inner door, and walk down the aisle.

When she did so, and looked up to find Caz staring at her as she was, any doubt she might have had, dissipated in an instant.

"She looks so beautiful," she whispered to her dad.

"Yes. Not as beautiful as you, mind, but I'm biased." He chuckled.

Caz sucked in a breath and gasped. "Jesus, she's stunning."

From Caz's viewpoint, she could tell Grace had done something fancy with her hair. The rich chocolate-brown of her hair, standing out beneath the starkly white veil. And there were flowers—lots of flowers—but mostly, it was the smile on Grace's face that did it for her.

That's what today was all about: Making her happy.

Dani leaned in, grinning. "Can't deny, you caught a hottie."

"Shut it, that's my wife you're leering at."

Just saying the words made it all so much easier to take in. A few more minutes and Grace *would* be her wife. That was a crazy thought, but a good one, she reminded herself.

When Mr Hart handed Grace off, Caz leaned in and found her eyes behind the veil.

"You look stunning," she murmured.

"So do you." Grace grinned.

The vicar coughed gently and got their attention. "Ladies and Gentlemen, Shes, Hes, Theys, and Thems, we are gathered here today—"

CHAPTER ONE

January 2024

"I want to have a baby."

That was the statement that started it all.

Grace sat in a chair in a coffee shop, with a mug of hot chocolate in her hand, and uttered those words aloud to her best friend, Caz.

"Right. Well, you'd better get on those dating apps then," Caz replied, a little glint in her eye as she sipped a matcha latte opposite her and picked grease from under her fingernail. There was always a stubborn bit that wouldn't wash out.

Grace stared at her for a moment, before her head tilted a little and she followed up her original statement with, "I want to have a baby...with you."

Had Caz not been blowing on her drink to cool it, she'd have spat it right out, spraying the entire table. Because, never in the almost twenty years they'd been friends, had Grace ever said anything like that.

"What?" She wiped her mouth on her sleeve, anyway, putting the mug down and buying herself some time to let the shock of it wear off to the point where she assumed Grace would laugh and say, *"Just kidding."* She didn't.

"I mean, I'm pretty sure you've noticed I do not have the body parts for that, and equally, I'm gay, you're not, and we're best friends." Caz pointed out what should have been bleeding obvious. Picking up her mug to hide behind, she took a sip, burnt her lip, and promptly began blowing again.

Grace shrugged. "I'm thirty-seven, and you're thirty-nine, and neither of us have ever had a better relationship than the one we have with each other."

"Which is because we don't have sex with each other and aren't attracted to one another," Caz said wisely.

She put her cup down once more and pulled the hair tie from her hair, gathering it all up and retying it in an act she knew bore out of nervousness more than the need to look tidy.

"I know," Grace concurred, "but that doesn't detract from the fact that, actually...I am at my happiest when I'm with you. And I can't think of another human being I'd want to help me raise a child. You'd be a great dad."

Caz wrinkled her nose. "I might work on cars for a living, and wear trousers and shirts—often a suit, I'll grant you, but I am not a man—"

"I don't mean you're a man. I mean, you'd be the one who took them to the park and ran around with them. You'd be the one they could talk with about football, or girls, and fix cars." She smiled. "You'd be the yin to my yang."

"Stop pulling my leg," Caz joked, but she didn't laugh. There was too much truth in those words. And Grace's face still didn't read like she was about to burst into laughter and shout, *"Gotcha!"*

"I'm deadly serious," Grace said, holding Caz captive with her eyes and the same steely determination she'd often seen in her best friend's stare. "Did you, or did you not, say that was the last Christmas you were spending trying to date?"

Caz fidgeted in her seat. "Yeah, because it's just nutters, kids, and more nutters on the prowl for hook-ups."

"Exactly. Whereas, you know what you're getting with me." She nodded, sure of everything she'd just said. "Stable. Steady. I've got a good job. We laugh so much. And I already know all your secrets."

Caz sat back and thought about it. Grace wasn't one to suggest something she wasn't serious about. And she wasn't wrong; they were happiest when it was just them. And romance was a big fat failure for them both thus far—but a baby?

Putting her cup down again, Caz leaned back in her seat. "Alright, hypothetically, let's say I agreed to this harebrained idea. How are you seeing it working?"

Grace smiled in the way that said she knew she might be winning.

"Well, obviously, we'd buy a house together. Big enough so we both had our own bedrooms, and then we'd just be a family like any other couple raising children."

"Just like that? No rules? No boundaries?" Caz picked up her mug again. Her drink was becoming a yo-yo in this conversation. "How would we work out bills? And what if you met someone and wanted to be with them? What about me and the child?"

"I'm not going to meet anyone," Grace said adamantly. "If we do this, I'll marry you and you'll be the official parent to said child."

"Fucking hell, Grace, marry? And never have sex again in my life?"

"You won't be having sex anyway. You're sworn off of dating." And then Grace shrugged nonchalantly. "We could have sex, or you could find someone to—"

"Woah, what? Say that again, more slowly so you can hear yourself talking utter nonsense."

"I said, we could—"

Caz held up a hand. "I can't have this conversation, Grace, it's madness."

"Is it, though? When you really think about it?" Grace leaned forward. "Between us, we earn a good wage. We would have the perfect house, a nice car, holidays abroad every year, and the family we both want." She sat back again. "We'd have each other."

"We already have each other."

Grace sighed. "So, what I'm not hearing, is a 'no'."

"No," Caz said firmly, but something in the back of her mind meant she had reason to pause. "No, you're not hearing a 'no'."

CHAPTER TWO

June 2025

"You may kiss...the bride," the vicar said with a smile.

Caz turned to Grace, and like they'd discussed and planned, and even practiced, she took Grace's face in her hands and planted one on her lips. Nothing too intimate, just a longer-than-usual peck, really, but the oohs and ahhs were perfectly attuned with the sound of cameras clicking and the flashes bursting into light around them, which, of course, made them smile.

"Alright?" Caz asked when Grace opened her eyes.

"Yeah." She beamed. "Ready to put on a show?"

"I am, Mrs..." Caz laughed and shook her head. "We'll figure it out."

The organ began again with the familiar Mendelssohn *Wedding March* playing them out, walking hand in hand as guests continued to take photos and stop them with words of congratulations, how beautiful they looked, and how they complimented one another.

It was easy to suspend reality and just go with it.

Outside, under the bright warm sunshine, the photographer moved them one way and another as he snapped all the group shots.

Then it was just them and the photographer. Everyone else had gone on ahead to the hotel where the reception would be held.

The venue was a swanky place that Ron, Grace's father, had insisted on paying for. Caz would have been happy with a few drinks at Blanca's, but she was, *Making Grace happy*, she kept reminding herself.

"Okay, so I was thinking a few candid shots of you both under this tree would work." The photographer looked up at the light dappled through the leaves. "Just there. Now, Caz, if you can get in as close as you can to Grace, and then just rest your forehead—" He waved a finger. "Perfect, and then both turn just a little to look at me—great." He snapped away.

"I feel a bit of dick," Caz said.

"Well, no different to usual then." Grace laughed, and Caz had to admit it was possibly true.

The photographer snapped away.

"Lovely, that's—yes... Okay, now, shall we do the kiss in front of that wooden arch?" He walked away towards it before either could say anything.

"More kissing." Caz laughed. "I've never kissed you before, and now—"

"You did kiss me once," Grace interrupted as they walked together, hand in hand, with their free hands lifting dresses from the grass.

"When?" Caz frowned.

"It was about four years ago. You'd had too much to drink after a party and I walked in. You were expecting that idiot..."

Caz wracked her brain for who she was dating four years ago and then grimaced. "Ugh, Valerie."

"Yeah, well it wasn't '*Ugh, Valerie*' then. But you thought I was her and...it was dark, and I'd had a fair bit to drink, too, and...you kissed me."

"Like...a kiss—"

"Yeah, the full snog." Grace laughed when Caz's face went beet red and her ears looked like they'd steam.

"Why didn't you tell me?"

Grace shrugged. "Didn't seem important. You'd have just been embarrassed, and I wasn't going to risk our friendship over it. It was no big deal... You didn't even remember the next day."

"Bloody hell."

"Want to take a moment?" the photographer asked. "Only, you both look a bit flushed." He grinned. "Understandable, it's hot and—" He thought better of whatever else he'd planned to say when Caz glared at him.

"I'm sorry," Caz said quietly to Grace.

Grace looked at her, confused. "About what?"

"Kissing you. That was... If you'd told me—" She went to run a hand through her hair and then remembered she was supposed to be looking her best.

Grace poked her. "Don't be stupid. It was ages ago, and I'd forgotten all about it 'til...well, 'til you kissed me in the church."

Caz rolled her eyes. "That wasn't really a kiss. That was just...a long peck."

"I know, but for some reason...it reminded me."

The photographer's voice interrupted, "Okay, so if we... alright, Grace, you turn around. Caz, scoot in really close, arms around Grace's waist."

They moved into position.

"So, was it good?" Caz asked against Grace's ear, grinning to herself.

"What?" Grace asked through her teeth as she smiled for the camera.

"The kiss. Was it good?" Caz whispered, but this time

Grace turned a little to look at her.

"In the church?" she said softly, their eyes holding each other's gaze.

"No," Caz laughed, "the proper kiss. Was it at least a good one?"

Grace giggled, shrugging at the same time. "I guess so. It's never been beaten."

"Wow, that good," Caz gloated. "Even better than Christopher Spencer?" He was the boy Grace had had a crush on in her teens, who had kissed her once and she'd never forgotten it.

"Shut up." Grace laughed, and as they became serious again for the photo, she said, "Yes, better than him."

They walked into the hall, still hand in hand. It was something neither of them had consciously thought about since they'd left the church. It just felt natural to them both to gravitate towards one another and always be connected. Plus, it didn't hurt the charade they were playing out.

A round of applause erupted, and whoops of excitement filled the air, along with several wolf whistles from Dani and the car crew.

"Here we go. Incoming," Caz whispered, spotting Grace's parents heading straight for them. "I'm gonna go and chat with the girls—let you have some time with them."

Their hands slid slowly apart as though their fingertips were not ready to detach. Eyes held on one another until Grace was tapped on the shoulder and turned to find a very happy face staring at her.

"Mum," Grace said, before one last glance over her shoulder at a retreating Caz. A glass of champagne was handed to her and she took a long gulp, still watching for where Caz had gone.

"Oh, Gracie, that was just...beautiful," her mum said, dabbing at her eyes. "Such a lovely service."

"It was, wasn't it? I don't really remember much." Grace laughed. Her eyes scanned the room. Caz had completely disappeared from her line of sight, and she felt the loss of her by her side.

"Don't worry, Sweetpea, it's all on video." Her dad leaned in and kissed her cheek. "Your wife already legged it?"

"Yeah, I think she's..." She looked around for a third time before, finally, she spotted the long dark hair through a window. "She's getting some air with her friends."

"I still can't believe it, really. Who'd have thought it—you and Caz after all these years." Ron chuckled.

"I know...took us by surprise, too," Grace said, still watching Caz. She smiled to herself when something Portia said made Caz laugh and her new wife's entire face lit up.

"Did it?" her mum asked seriously, and Grace brought her attention back to the room. "I mean, I know you've never been gay, but, I dunno, I always thought there was something about Caz that just...fit with you."

"Really?" She caught sight of Caz through the window again, only this time, Caz was looking back. They shared a smile. "I suppose we have always been thick as thieves."

"And the rest," her mum laughed, "I thought she'd moved in with us at one point, she was there so often."

"Was she? I don't remember that."

"Ron, what did we say about Caz that summer? You

remember?"

"We said, 'At this rate, we'll have to start charging rent.'"

They both laughed and Grace smiled, but her attention was still on Caz, laughing again with her work bestie, Dani. Fooling everyone into thinking they were a real couple was going to be a piece of cake if her own parents bought it.

"I'm just going to...find my wife."

"Good plan. Dinner will be served in a few minutes." Her dad glanced at his watch and nodded. "I'm starving. Couldn't eat a thing this morning—I was that nervous."

"Oh, Dad, you are sweet."

"Only gonna happen this once. I couldn't mess it up for you, Sweetpea."

"Never." She kissed his cheek then gave her mum a quick hug. "Go get settled, I'll find Caz."

Outside, the fresh air was welcome. She waved to Caz, who spoke quietly to Dani and then walked away from her group of friends towards Grace.

"Everything alright?"

"Yes, darling," Grace said, as another small group bundled outside for cigarettes, passing them. When they were out of earshot, she said, "Dinner is about to be served and we need to be in place, ready for speeches."

"God, I forgot about those." Caz shook visibly. "I'm winging it. I couldn't write a single thing that made any sense... or didn't give it all away."

Grace kissed her cheek. "You'll be fine. You're good on your toes."

"I am—you're right," Caz said, filled with confidence in an instant, just from a few words. "See, this is why we're the perfect match."

"I know." Grace laughed. "Come on, let's go show each other off."

CHAPTER THREE

January 2024

The wine was good, the beer was cold, and the TV was off. But unlike any other Saturday night in together, this was far from usual.

Caz sat in the armchair, leaning forward, both elbows on her knees as she reeled off questions for Grace to answer.

Important things like, "Where are we going to live?"

"Buy a house on the outskirts of town. We've both got good finances. We'd get a mortgage easily," Grace answered. She had answers for everything.

"And we'd tell everyone what? That we're sad old farts who have given up on love, so we've settled for each other?"

Grace huffed. "I don't see it as settling. I see it as we're never going to find anyone else who brings what we do to this relationship—"

"Except sex and intimacy?" Caz choked out. "That's important, surely?"

"Yes, and I think we could be—"

"Do not say it," Caz said, standing quickly and walking to the window. She turned suddenly. "You're straight. It's not like hooking up with a bloke down at the pub, there will be feelings involved—platonic maybe—but still, feelings and emotions, and..." She moved to crouch in front of Grace. "Can you honestly say you've never considered sex with a woman?"

"I've considered it, yes..."

"And?"

"I decided it wasn't for me, but—"

"See? So how do you propose we get around that?" Caz stood up and went back to the chair, flopping down into it.

"If you'd let me speak." Grace glared, and then relaxed when Caz smiled apologetically. "I think we already share an intimacy, one of trust and love, and emotional attachment, and that if we wanted it to, could maybe turn into a more physical—" She held up a warning finger when Caz went to interrupt again. "We hug all the time. We snuggle up together and watch films, and don't think I haven't noticed how you take care of me when we're out."

Caz sat up straighter.

"Think I don't notice the little guiding touches to the small of my back, or my elbow, or how you put yourself between me and any potential danger? We *are* intimate, it's just not a sexual intimacy...and no, I couldn't consider sex with women in general, but maybe, in time...I could with you. Because you're you, and not just any woman."

This time Caz sat silently.

"You're my person, Caz. And that means more to me than any man ever will."

Caz felt her eyes moisten and blinked it away. Wasn't that just the kind of thing she'd been waiting her entire life for someone to say to her?

For someone to really see her?

"But what if you met *that* man? What if we did this, and we had a baby, and two years—three years—down the line, Prince Charming waltzes in?"

"That is a fear of abandonment that could happen to anyone, in any relationship. I am saying I'd make a commitment to you. I wouldn't be looking to meet Prince Charming."

"But I could have a hook-up situationship?"

"If having sex regularly with another lesbian means that much to you, then yes, I'd be okay with that."

"I wouldn't," Caz balked.

"Then what are you arguing? I don't get it."

Caz gulped down the wine. "I'm not arguing anything, I'm just thinking out loud, I suppose, and I think it's best to get these questions out there, don't you? I mean, won't you miss sex?"

"Honestly, what I get from men, I can do myself with my trusty iVibe." Grace grinned. "Generally, a better job and less complaining, and doesn't need to be fed or cleaned for."

Caz laughed. "I mean, that right there is a reason to marry a woman." She went quiet for a moment, before brown eyes met the other brown eyes across the room. They were going to do this, weren't they? "What would we tell everyone?"

"The truth. That we've realised there is nobody else we'd rather be with for the rest of our lives."

"I don't think people will get it."

"Who cares if they get it?" Grace asked.

Caz shrugged. "I guess, I do."

Grace sighed. "Then we will act like a couple. Let them see what they want to see. And in every aspect of normal day-to-day things, we *would* be a couple."

Caz thought about all the times when people would ask if they were together. She'd never really understood it, but now, with Grace pointing things out, she wondered if it really was such a crazy idea, especially after Grace spoke again.

"I love you. And you love me. And I don't want to be knocking on fifty and wondering why my life ended up miserable when we have the opportunity to have it all."

"Including a baby?"

Grace looked at her friend for a long moment. When she hadn't spoken, Caz gave her 'the look' the one that said, "Well?"

"Yes," Grace finally said. "I want a baby, maybe even two, I don't know, but I'm thirty-seven and the likelihood of that happening naturally is pretty slim, and I don't want to take any chances and end up—"

"Knocking on fifty and miserable?"

Grace smiled. "Yeah, and I think...even if I were doing that on my own, you'd be the surrogate parent anyway, wouldn't you?"

Caz shrugged again. "Well, yeah, I'm not going to let you do it on your own, am I? That's what friends are for, right?"

"Right. And you would be round my place every night after work to make sure I had support, was watered and fed, and generally taking care of the baby so I could nap, or have a bath, or —"

"Alright, fine, yes, I'd make the perfect parent," Caz laughed, "but then I'd go home and live my life away from you and the baby, and you'd eventually start to get your life back and —"

"You could still live your life if we were married. I'm not going to be stopping you from doing whatever you want to do."

"Yeah, I know."

"The question is: Do you want to have a baby...with me? Or anyone? It's a huge decision and one I don't take lightly in asking."

Caz dropped her head into her hands and stared at the floor.

"I don't know that it has ever been something I'd considered possible before, but with you? I dunno. It feels like everything just slots into place and I can't imagine not having a baby..." glancing up, she added, "with you."

Grace's face lit up, but she still said, "It's okay if you don't want—"

"I do. I think we should do it."

Grace grinned. "You do?"

Caz nodded. "Yeah, I mean...you're right, there's no reasonable argument for why we shouldn't."

"Except sex?" Grace raised a brow. "Obviously, I get it that sleeping with me isn't—"

"Sleeping with you isn't the problem. I could, with time and reciprocal interest, maybe move our relationship in that direction. But I'm aware you're straight, and sleeping with me would just be you doing what you think I want, and not because you actually want to sleep with me, and that just feels accommodating, not hot and sexy, which is what I'd need."

Grace remained silent. There wasn't really much she could add without it getting weirder than it already was.

"So, what do we do now?" Caz finally asked.

"Call a family meeting and explain—"

"Nope." Caz stood up. "No, I'm not...I don't want everyone thinking we're a couple of saddos who can't find anyone to love us." She turned to face Grace. "Because you're right, we do love each other."

"Right. So...we tell them that." Grace stood up.

"Yeah...but..." Caz moved towards her. "Do you think they'll buy it?"

"That me and you love each other?" Grace nodded. "Yeah,

I think they would. Friends fall in love with each other all the time, don't they?"

"I guess...we'd have to be a bit more tactile."

Grace wrapped her palm around Caz's bicep. "We already are..."

"They're going to ask questions and probably want proof. It's going to be—"

"Weird, I know, but nothing we can't handle. You're my person, Caz, I know that for sure," she chuckled, "and ya not ugly. It's not like it's a chore to pretend I fancy you now."

"Oh, you'd fancy me for sure if you was gay," Caz joked.

"I would. Absolutely." Grace laughed, her hand sliding down Caz's arm to take her hand. "Just like you'd fancy me, so... we're a perfect match."

CHAPTER FOUR

June 2025

"If you'd asked me five years ago who I thought I'd see my Sweetpea marrying, I'd have said he'd be a playboy type that caused her nothing but trouble." Ron Hart grinned. "But if you'd asked me a year ago if I thought young Caz here would sweep her off her feet and they'd finally admit their feelings for one another...I'd have said we kind of had an idea..."

Caz blushed. Grace laughed and leaned in, kissing her cheek. "Sorry," she whispered, allowing Caz to turn to her. To the watching crowd it looked like two lovers sharing a moment, and they *were* sharing a moment.

"I can handle it, they're all buying it. That, and you having the best day, that's what matters."

Grace blushed and her smile widened.

"The thing is, in all seriousness, if you'd asked us to pick the perfect person to love our Sweetpea, to take care of her, support her through all the trials and tribulations that life and marriage will bring, we'd have chosen Caz too." He stopped speaking and raised his glass. "So, without further ado, I hope you'll all join me in toasting these two and wishing them all the best for a wonderful and happy life together."

The entire room chorused together as Caz smiled at Grace once more. "You've gotta kiss me." She chuckled.

"Hardship." Grace laughed and planted a peck on her lips again. "See?" She giggled, pulling away slowly. "Your turn."

"Huh?" Caz frowned. "How many kisses do you need?"

"No, dimwit." Grace laughed and leaned in close. "Speech?"

Caz's eyes went wide. "Oh, shit, I forgot." She stood up and tapped her glass with the edge of a knife to get everyone's attention.

"Hi, if I can—hi," she said, glancing around the room at all of their friends and families. Looking down at Grace, she felt the nerves ease when a hand slid into hers. "So, I didn't write a speech, I figured I'd wing it."

A ripple of laughter further eased her nerves.

"Thing is, if you'd asked me five years ago if I'd be here, marrying my best friend, I'd have laughed and agreed with Ron —she'd have been dating a playboy."

"Hey," Grace gasped playfully.

More laughter.

"But...thankfully, she saw sense, and somehow, we found a way to work out that we are perfect for each other." She turned to face Grace. "And if I had to pick one person on this planet to spend the rest of my days with...the honest answer is, it would be her."

Grace blushed again and smiled up at her.

"So, before we all starve to death, I'd like to raise a toast to my wife, Grace. My person."

Once more a chorus erupted, along with a round of applause as Caz sat down.

"That was beautiful," Grace said. Watery eyes looked right into Caz's soul.

"I know. They're lapping it up, too." Caz laughed, and without warning kissed Grace, to another chorus of congratulations. "Sorry, I—"

"It's fine, you don't have to ask. You're my wife,

remember?" Grace smiled, before her attention was taken by a waiter leaning over her other shoulder to place a plate down on the table in front of her.

"Okay, food," Caz said, rubbing her hands together. "I am famished." But the words, *My wife,* repeated over and over in her head.

They'd practiced the dance. Firstly, because Caz wasn't quite as graceful as Grace when it came to moving in time, and with someone else.

And secondly, Grace had always been led, which meant Caz had to learn to do that too, and then they'd had to work out how they could make it look intimate and real in front of all of their loved ones, without actually having to do anything that made the other feel uncomfortable.

The song choice had taken a while to settle on, of course. They'd batted lots of options back and forth, but in the end they'd both agreed on Ed Sheeran's *Perfect.* Because it was just that: Perfect.

The words were beautiful, and in some ways it encapsulated the two of them. They'd fallen in friend-love when they were kids, when Grace was nineteen and Caz was almost twenty-one, working together at the garage while Grace finished her studies.

Thick as thieves they'd been, right from the start. And Ron hadn't minded. It was good to have his daughter working in the office and not frolicking with the lads who worked for him.

There were dalliances of course, but nobody ever stuck around. Not like Caz. And none of the boys would dare step out of line—not because their boss was Grace's dad, but because Caz would string 'em up and rip 'em a new one if she found out. And she would find out, because Grace would tell her. They told each other everything.

Now here they were, on the dance floor by themselves, looking shyly at one another as they met in the middle, and Grace slid her arms up and around Caz's neck. Reciprocating hands attached to her waist as the music gave way to lyrics, and they swayed and turned and held each other's gaze, smiling at one another, whispering quietly to one another about their guests and the day.

Grace laughed when Caz spontaneously sung, "*Darling you look perfect, tonight.*" Caz pulled Grace closer, and then as rehearsed, spun her out and back in again, much to the crowd's enjoyment. It all felt so real…and intimate.

There was no way they weren't pulling this off.

And when it was halfway through and everyone else joined them on the dance floor, they stood still, hands clasped between them, as they stared at one another, each swaying gently with their own unasked questions.

The music came to a halt, everyone applauded, and the pair of them scarpered, running up the stairs, giggling.

"Caz, wait." Grace laughed, stopping mid-flight to kick off her heels. And then she was running again to catch up. "Okay, go. Have you got the key?"

Caz reached into her dress and plucked the key card from her bra. "Yup."

Their room was on the first floor and was the one everyone getting married used. No way around that without looking suspicious. But what did it matter there was only one bed?

They'd slept in worse places together, including several of the back seats of Caz's cars after a night out when they'd drunk too much and couldn't drive back.. And who could forget when they'd gone on a mad trip to Blackpool just to ride the Big One, before driving back home. There had been numerous times they'd woken up on a sofa, snuggled into each other under a blanket, having fallen asleep watching a film.

"I dunno how you can wear dresses all day," Caz said when the door shut behind them. She pulled a hair tie off her wrist and swept her hair up, turning her back to Grace as she wriggled free of her dress and tossed it onto the bed.

"Unzip me?" Grace said.

Caz turned, in just her underwear, lacy stuff she would not have picked had it not been for Grace talking about VPL. Caz had needed to google that, and read that outfits with a 'visible panty line' might require no underwear, so a compromise was made and her usual shorts-style was put to one side for the dress.

Sweeping Grace's long plait to the side, she tried to grab the fiddly little zipper. "Bloody hell, why do they make these so small?" Her free hand landed on Grace's bare shoulder for balance.

When she finally got hold of the zip, Caz muttered, "Slippery little—" and slid it downwards, revealing Grace. She glanced up and noticed both of them in the full-sized mirror.

Eyes connected through the glass.

"I know everyone's said it to you today, but you really do look beautiful," Caz said over her shoulder. She continued to watch as Grace remained quiet, only moving to twist the ring now on her finger. "Are you alright?"

Grace nodded. "Yes, just really understanding that I know I did the right thing." She smiled. "We are perfect."

"Yeah, I think we are," Caz answered. "So, get changed so we can dance the night away, get drunk, and fall into that bed for a really, really deserved sleep."

"Sleep?" Grace said, turning back to face Caz, her eyes quickly scanning the half-naked body in front of her. "You don't want to have—"

Caz's eyes widened like saucers as she found her voice unable to speak.

"Oh, my God, your face." Grace giggled. She pulled her arms free of the dress and continued to laugh. "Sorry, that was mean of me."

"Yeah, it was," Caz smiled, "and dangerous...one day I might take you up on an offer like that." She turned towards the wardrobe and opened the door, changing the angle of the mirror.

"You would not," Grace said, completely sure of herself.

"Try again later when I've had a few...apparently, that's when I forget who I'm kissing."

Now it was Grace who turned beet red. "God, I should never have told you that."

"Too late. Now I know I'm the best snog you've ever had, I am totally taking those bragging rights."

Grace wiggled her hips until the dress fell to the floor and surrounded her like a great white puddle of silky protection.

"You are a git."

"I'm your git, though." Caz turned and held out a hanger with Grace's suit.

"That is true. You are. You can't escape now."

Caz laughed. "Well, duh."

"You know we can't just get changed and go down again. We need to waste some time, so they'll all be assuming we're up here getting it on."

Caz dropped her arm and huffed. "Wanna watch some TV?"

"Might as well. Mini-Bar?"

"Go on, then." Caz laughed and found a T-shirt from earlier to pull on. Then she launched herself at the bed and lifted the covers, slid under, and found the remote.

"Beer or wine?" Grace asked, still in her underwear.

For a moment, Caz wondered if this is what her real wedding day should have looked like, had she married someone gay and totally into her, of course. She closed her eyes at the image that moved through her head in that moment and said a quiet, "Beer, please."

CHAPTER FIVE

March 2024

Grace sat nervously at the table in her small flat and looked at the three other faces sitting around it, all looking at her expectantly. Was this what Caz had to go through every time she met someone new and had to come out of the closet again?

She'd invited them over. The intention being to tell them about the new turn in her relationship with Caz.

These were her oldest friends, those first-day-of-school pals who had known her forever, and if she couldn't convince them about Caz, then there was no way she'd convince anyone else.

"Well, this is fun," Cressida said, raising her wine glass to sip demurely. "Are we going to find out the big secret?"

Grace laughed. "It's not a secret, I just…it might surprise you, that's all."

Sandra smiled. "I've got an evening off from Greg and the kids—surprise away."

"Alright." Grace took a deep breath. "So, you all know my friend Caz, right?"

"Yes, the mechanic who looks like she's been cast in a movie about mechanics?" Sandra said with an impish grin. When everyone else turned to look at her, she laughed. "What? You don't think she has a 'Julia Roberts joins *Fast and Furious*' vibe to her?"

"I can see that, actually," Grace said, beaming, before

remembering what she'd started saying. "Anyway, yes, her...that Caz." She took a large glug from her wine and placed the glass down again slowly. "The thing is, Caz and I, we've been close for a long time and things have—"

"I knew it! Didn't I say it?" Cressida jumped up and clapped her hands. "Jane, what did I say?"

"Well, we don't actually know what Grace is telling us yet," Jane, the quieter, more thoughtful one of the group, answered.

Cressida pursed her lips but sat down.

"So, yes, Caz and I, we're together, as in, a couple, as in, going to move in together..."

"Can I gloat now?" Cressida said to Jane, before turning back to Grace. "It took you this long to see it? I can't believe I noticed first."

"What did you notice?" Grace asked, suddenly aware of the fact Cressida was very insistent about the relationship.

"Oh, come on, it was obvious. You two have been joined at the hip for years. I always thought, if one of us was going to try the gay path, it would be you, with Caz."

Sandra nodded. "I thought you already were, and just didn't want to say anything."

"Really? Why?" Grace asked, absolutely intrigued by this. She was all prepared to sit and fight her corner, but apparently, they'd always assumed it anyway.

Three sets of shoulders shrugged.

"You've always been close with each other, it just kind of seemed natural it would have developed," Jane said. "And we're happy for you." She looked at the others, who all nodded and smiled.

"As long as you're happy, and judging by how you are anytime Caz is around, it would appear you are," Sandra chipped in.

"I am," Grace admitted. "Caz is my person. She just gets me, and we want the same things, and there isn't anyone I'd rather be doing life with than her."

"Moving in together—that's serious," Cressida added.

"I think it's about time." Sandra laughed. "You said yourself, it's like they've been dating for years."

Jane reached for her drink. "So, now that's out of the way, what else shall we talk about?"

"Grace?" Dani blurted, as common now as she had been when Caz had met her in sixth form at Bath Street Secondary. Thankfully, her pint glass was on the table and she hadn't taken a mouthful yet. "You and Grace?"

"Yes, Grace." Caz rolled her eyes. You'd think she'd just told them she was moving in with a man. "It's not that shocking," she added, staring at them all.

Dani sat, open mouthed, one side of her hair hanging long, the other shaved off. Portia and Dalilah, both in suits, hair slicked and held in place with God only knew how many products, looked impassive.

It always tickled Caz how the butchest women she knew could both have such girly names.

Portia leaned in, pushed her thick-framed glasses up her nose and then ran a hand through the two inches of hair on her head as she said in her cut-glass English accent—a gift from boarding school and a degree at Cambridge, "To be fair, she's quite...straight."

"And as we all know, sexuality is fluid," Caz reminded

them.

"So, like…you've always been together, or is this like, a new thing?" Dalilah asked. She had more of a Brummie accent, seeing as her parents had settled there when they'd immigrated from India three decades ago. It had softened over time as she'd been living down south since her own uni days at Brighton.

"It's a new thing," Caz answered. "We've always been close, so you could say we've kind of been dating all along, but now we're…" She didn't want to lie to her friends, so she picked her words carefully. "We talked and realised we both think we're the perfect match for each other."

"And what? You had too much to drink one night and snogged her? Like, how did this come about?" Dani piped up, a little less shocked now she'd had time to absorb the information.

Caz felt uneasy. "You know what it's like—you've been friends for years and then suddenly, you look at them differently, and you already know what you both want from life and so, it's easy to just step over that line and—"

"But…" Portia broke in again, "she's never been with a woman before, has she?"

Caz sat back. "I have far too much respect for Grace than to be discussing her previous relationships. I'm not asking for permission from you all, or even expecting any of you to understand. I just have respect for you guys, too, and I wanted to share my news with you all."

Dalilah grinned. "You're right. It's none of our business. We're happy for you, right guys?"

Dani and Portia both nodded.

"Good…cos we're moving in together."

"Okay…bit quick, init?" Dani stammered out.

Portia stood up. "I think we need more drinks. Same,

again?"

Three heads nodded and she wandered off towards the bar.

"I get it, you've known her for years, but so have we and we aint..." Dani's face scrunched up at the idea, "...don't you want to see if things work out now you've...you know, added in intimacy?"

Caz frowned. "You know, I don't remember you being so diligent when you met Paula, or Sinead, or who was that other one?"

Dalilah chipped in with a mischievous grin, "Nerys."

"I didn't move in with them," Dani exclaimed a little too defensively.

"You might as well have. You got engaged after a week with Sinead and after a month with Paula. You barely knew them. Grace and I have been tight for nearly twenty years."

"Yeah, which is why it's weird that all of a sudden you're into each other," Dani pointed out.

Caz shrugged. "So, we're different people now... ready to settle down and just enjoy life."

Dani raised her hands in acceptance. "Alright."

"Okay, here we go. One for you," Portia said, placing a pint glass in front of Caz, "and you, and you, and me." She grinned. When they all had a drink in their hands, she said, "Congratulations, Caz. Wishing you and Grace all the best."

"Hear, hear." Dalilah raised her glass to the centre for them all to clink together.

"To you and Grace," Dani said.

"Thank guys, it means a lot that you're all okay with it," Caz said after she'd sipped her drink. "Not that it would change anything, but you know, it's good to have your friends on your side, right?"

"Hell, yeah, it is." Dalilah laughed. "Always, Caz, always."

Opening the door, Grace smiled. "So, how did it go?" She moved aside and let Caz in.

Her best friend shrugged nonchalantly. "As expected. They were a bit shocked I'd snagged the straight girl, especially because they thought it would have happened by now. She shrugged again. "But they're happy for us... You?"

"Weirdly, mine were the opposite. They thought we'd been shagging the entire time and had just been waiting for me to tell them."

Caz raised a brow at that. "Really? Why?"

Now it was Grace who shrugged. "Apparently, we have always been *'joined at the hip'* and if any of us were to be trying out the gay path, they thought it would be me."

Caz pressed her lips together to suppress the laughter. "You're like the least gay person I know."

"I know, right?" Grace joined in with the giggles. "I don't know whether to be offended or not." She laughed, harder this time.

"At least we have them all convinced."

"Yeah, that's the main thing." Grace grinned. "Tea?"

CHAPTER SIX

April 2024

Caz's phone rang. She pushed the trolley with her feet and came out from under a Ford Focus. The blue overalls that should have been covering her arms and torso were casually rolled down to her waist, the arms tied across her stomach, oil drips all down her clothing.

Before she jumped up, Frank handed her the phone.

"Cheers." She smiled at him, before hitting the answer button. "Hello."

"Hey, it's me…listen, there's a house literally just about to go on the market I think is perfect for us. Pete called from the Woodington office and gave me the heads up. I've just got back and it is…perfect." She barely paused for breath and Caz had to smile at her excitement. "Three bedrooms, two bathrooms, large kitchen, dining room, and lounge, with a small garden and parking for two. It's in Banbury Hollow. Can you go and look at it?"

"I thought we were looking at Amberfield?" Caz checked her watch. "Grace, you know I'm working till four. I can whizz over then, I suppose."

"Great, I'll add you to the diary and have Pete meet you there."

"How much is it?" Caz asked, pushing herself up onto her feet and strolling over to the bench where a half-empty can of Coke stood going flat.

There was silence for a moment and she swigged the

drink, grimacing, but going back for seconds.

"Grace, how much?" She wiped her mouth against the back of her hand and inadvertently smeared grease across her chin.

"Okay, hear me out. It's over our budget, but I really think we could—"

"Grace?"

"Three seven five," Grace said, and Caz could imagine her wincing with every word uttered.

"Three hundred and seventy-five thousand of our British pounds?" Caz exclaimed with just an edge of incredulity to her voice. "Babe, we worked this out. With mine and your savings, plus our earnings, we can just about scrape three fifty."

"I know, but they're eager to sell and I'm pretty sure they'd take an offer, and Dad said he wants to give us ten grand as a wedding gift."

"What? We're not getting married for another year."

"I know...but he's happy for us and he wants to help, so... can you?"

"Can I what?"

"Go and look at it," Grace said impatiently. "And if you like it, tell Pete you want to make an offer and go in with three thirty-five."

"That's nowhere near the asking price."

"Of course not, but we're not going in with everything we have, there's a negotiation to be done."

"Just feels mean," Caz said, scratching her head before wiping her hands down the front of her white vest.

Frank looked at her and shook his head. She shrugged.

"Right, fine. I will go and take a look after I've been home for a shower."

"That's all I ask," Grace said sweetly. "Thank you."

"You're welcome. What time will you be home later? I'll come over."

"Finishing at seven."

"Great, I'll pick up something for dinner then." She glanced around and found Dani staring at her, with Ron stood right there too. "Okay, baby, can't wait to get off…I mean, finish, and see you."

"Who's there? Is it Dad?"

"Uh-huh. So, I'll catch you later, yep, okay…yes, love you, too, bye." Caz closed the phone before Grace's laughter became so loud the entire building heard her.

Ron gave her a proud smile and a thumbs up.

"Is this almost done? Customers on the phone," Dani said, chewing gum like a snapping alligator.

"Yeah, just got to refill the oil chamber and give it a run for ten minutes—make sure the seals are good."

"Great, I'll tell her four, then."

"Okie dokie." Caz grinned just as her phone buzzed.

Grace: Love you too! Hahahaha

"Git," Caz muttered before shoving the phone back into her pocket and dropping back down onto the trolley. But she grinned and murmured as she slid back under the car, "My git."

From the outside it looked nice enough.

There was a red door at the front and to the right of the

building, with a little roof to shield you from the rain while you tried to get a key into the lock and open it. To the left of that was a large bay window, with two more windows above.

It was detached, with room for two cars to park out front —exactly how Grace described it.

"So, it literally came on the market this morning. We haven't even done the photos yet, but Grace had already given us all the heads up on what you guys were looking for." Pete smiled at her as he pushed the key into the lock and turned it.

"Yeah, she seems pretty excited about it."

They stepped inside to a long hallway. A set of stairs led up the right side, with wooden flooring all the way through.

Clean, tidy, and potentially perfect.

"Alright, well to the left here is the lounge. Double aspect windows and door through to the dining room. A wood burner in the fireplace is working and all up to standard," Pete explained, as Caz wandered around the empty room.

"Nobody lives here, then?"

"Nope. Basically, they're a couple and they both had a property, so, living in the other and selling this one."

"That's nice." Caz smiled and poked her head into the dining room. "It's not a divorce or...someone died?"

Pete chuckled, before continuing on, "Single aspect window—not the biggest, but certainly sizeable for a decent table and chairs."

The dining room led through to the kitchen. Nothing fancy, but liveable. Units lined two walls into the corner, a breakfast bar protruded from a third wall, and a door led out to the garden behind it, with another door leading full circle, back into the hallway.

She glanced out of the window and saw a small, tidy

grassed area. She imagined Grace out there, looking back at her and waving, belly swollen with a baby, a toddler running around her legs, laughing, and Caz felt a sensation of pride and love rush through her.

"So, all doable," Pete was saying.

"Sorry, what was that?"

"Oh, I was saying it doesn't really need much, maybe just change the décor...all doable?" He smiled. "Want to see upstairs?"

"Yeah, I guess...I'm not really an expert, though."

"No, that's Grace's forte. She's had a definite spring in her step lately, too... All down to you I guess."

"Oh, well, then I suppose I must have a spring in my step, too, then."

"Indeed. Shall we go on?"

So far, Caz noted, every wall was either white or a muted pastel, and she quite liked it as it was, imagining Grace's corner sofa in the lounge and her own TV on the wall. It was easy to imagine them living here, but she didn't want to get hers or Grace's hopes up. They were well away, financially.

She followed him out into the hall again, noting a smaller room off to the side of the kitchen with a desk and bookcase, an office of some kind. With a Harry Potter style cupboard under the stairs with room for hoovers and other annoying things nobody wanted to look at, and a tiny toilet and shower room squeezed into a space that backed onto the dining room.

"There are three bedrooms upstairs, though that office space downstairs could also be used as a living space of any kind," he said, climbing the stairs two at a time.

Caz jogged up behind him.

They'd need safety gates, that was for sure, she thought.

"Okay, single room straight ahead, then the first double to the left of that, bathroom with full suite and shower, and then the master bedroom to the front."

She moved easily into each room, imagining her bedroom in one, Grace's room in the other, and a child sleeping soundly in the small room.

Grace was right; there was nothing not to like.

"So, where do we stand with the buyers? Grace said they're looking for a quick move?"

Clasping his clipboard to his chest, Pete nodded sagely. "Yep. They've found a property abroad they want to buy as a holiday home, but there are time constraints. So—

"A deal is to be made?"

"Precisely."

"Okay…so, I can make an offer now and—"

"I will call them up and let them know, then it's up to them to agree or not. What figure were you thinking?"

Caz puffed out her cheeks. She hated dealing with money, especially when it felt a bit underhanded, but Grace was the expert so she trusted the process.

"What about a cheeky three three five?" She tried to sound confident and make sure she looked like she knew what the game was.

Pete grinned and pulled his phone out. "I'll give them a call." He was already walking away, phone to his ear. She heard him exuberantly say, "Hey, Kathy, yes, it's Pete from Osgood's, uh-huh, yes, I do—"

Caz walked to the back of the house and looked out of the bedroom window into the garden. It had a nice patio area where a table and chairs could sit, maybe a barbecue. They'd have their friends round and sit out in the sunshine with a paddling pool.

"Okay, so they're going to have a think about it," Pete said, coming back into the room.

"Not a no, then?"

"I'll be honest, I expect a no, but the fact they're thinking about it tells me we might not be too far off it."

CHAPTER SEVEN

June 2025

Finally, Caz felt like herself again. Standing in front of the mirror, she adjusted the jacket of her suit and the collar on her shirt.

"I don't know why you haven't been snapped up by a hot lesbian," Grace said from over her shoulder. Once more, they watched each other through the glass. "I mean, you're literally everything a girl would want: Kind and loyal, funny..." She winked. "Sometimes."

"Hey, I am funny *all* the time."

"Maybe that's the problem—your jokes put them off," Grace laughed, "whereas, I've known you for so long, they're quite endearing now."

"Cheek of it." Caz smiled at her.

The air grew still as they continued to stare at one another, a comfortable silence between them. There were moments during their friendship when Caz *did* wonder if they'd be able to cross that line. It was the subtle stuff, nothing too loud, just a little echo of something she could never quite label, but it was there. She was sure she hadn't imagined it.

She'd always ignored it, pushed it away, and not allowed her curiosity to ruin their friendship. But every now and then, Grace would say something. It wasn't so much *what* she said, but the *way* she said it, and it would pique a question: *Did Grace have the same curiosity?*

"Right, enough faffing, we have a party to attend." Grace

grinned and headed for the door. She stopped and looked back. "Come on, we've already given them enough time to imagine what we've been up to."

"I'm not sure how I feel about that."

Grace stopped and frowned. "What?"

"I mean...people...people like your mum and dad, imagining what we've been up to...it's a tad creepy, isn't it?"

The frown turned into a grimace. "Well, when you put it like that."

Caz laughed. "I need a drink to wash that thought away."

"You've already had two beers and a scotch and Coke."

"Ooh...married for all of..." she checked her watch, "five hours, and she's counting my drinks already."

Grace hit her playfully. "Dead right, I am. You snore when you're drunk."

"I do not," Caz said in mock offence as she yanked the door open. "How dare you suggest such a thing."

"I'll record you ton—"

"Alright, lovebirds, what you been up to, eh?" It was one of Grace's cousins, slightly worse for wear, so it was clear what he'd been doing.

Grace smiled at him, then very demurely said, "Just watching TV, Ken."

He laughed nervously but said nothing more when Caz raised her brows at him.

"Don't be mean," Grace said, tugging her hand.

"What? I said nothing."

Grace pulled her close. "You didn't have to. You know how easily you intimidate people."

Caz grinned.

"Only when you're the reason," Dani said, sneaking up and poking her head between them. "She's not interested otherwise."

"Oh, really, it's just my honour she defends?" Grace went along with the gentle ribbing. "I didn't know that. I thought she was grouchy with everyone."

"Nah, only those daring to give you any—"

"I am not intimidating, they are intimidated. There is a difference," Caz said, just a little defensively.

Grace flung her arms around her and said, "I'm not complaining."

"See, grouchy?" Dani chuckled.

"Why are you here?" Caz asked her friend. "This isn't your floor."

"I was just nosing around, seeing how the other half live." Dani winked. "Posh init?"

Caz ignored her, and Grace smiled. It was posh, that was true.

"Well, I'm going to get a drink while you two work out which one's getting the grouchy version of me next." Caz poked out her tongue and turned away.

Dani laughed. "That'll be me, then."

"Make mine a double," Grace called after her.

They stood together, Caz's two closest friends, and watched as she walked towards the bar.

"It was a lovely service," Dani said. "You looked beautiful, by the way."

"Thanks. I don't remember much. It was all just a blur of focusing on not falling over and saying the right lines." Grace chuckled. "It's all so serious."

"Worth it though, right? You two look so happy, it makes me wonder if I should settle down."

Grace smiled, her line of sight still on Caz. Someone had stopped her and she was laughing at whatever they said. Those candid moments, when Grace saw sides of Caz she'd never really paid much attention to before, always made her feel...home?

"Honestly, it might be the most sensible thing I've ever done," Grace admitted. "Would you excuse me? I just need to powder my nose, as they say in the movies." Because she needed a moment, away from it all, and not watching her wife.

They'd cut the cake, eaten more buffet food than anyone possibly should, and danced their socks off, all the while sinking glasses of alcoholic beverages and telling everyone that asked just how happy they were, and not once did they slip up.

But now, at ten to midnight, Caz slurred, "Think we should go up?"

"Yes." Grace sagged against her. "I am so tired."

"Come on then." Caz took her hand and tugged, almost knocking someone over as she staggered. "Oops, sorry," she laughed, "taking my wife to bed."

A chorus of rowdy responses followed, and Grace even had the decency to blush, but she didn't stop to respond, following Caz up the stairs again, just like they'd done a few hours ago.

At the door to their room, Caz fell against it and fumbled in her pockets for the card.

"Can't find it," she said.

Grace rolled her eyes. "It was in your pocket."

"I know but...can't...find..."

Slapping her hands away, Grace moved in, delving the fingers of her right hand into Caz's pocket, holding her upright with the other hand.

"Will you stand still?" Grace giggled.

"You're tickling." Caz wriggled. Eventually, Grace pulled the card free and shoved it into the lock. The tiny click unlocked the door and she pulled the handle, the door opening and Caz almost toppling into the room.

"Am so drunk." Caz chuckled. She staggered towards the bed and landed on it, face down. "Sleep here."

"Oh no you don't," Grace said, moving to shut the door and then cross to where Caz lay with her feet hanging off the bed by a foot. "Not quite how I planned my wedding night all those years ago, but…" She sighed and grabbed the first of Caz's shoes. Yanking it free, she dropped it to the ground and pulled off the other one.

"Come and cuddle," Caz said, though her face was mushed against the bedding and it sounded a lot more like, "Um and uddle."

"You need to get undressed and into pyjamas."

When Caz rolled over, Grace thought she might be getting somewhere, but no, Caz just lay there until the snoring began.

"Caroline Iris Madden, you wake up right now and get undressed," Grace said sternly, hands on hips.

Caz jumped up. "Huh, what?"

Laughing, Grace repeated what she'd said, minus the full name part, but it did make her giggle again.

"Alright, I'm getting—" Her arms came up and the jacket was shrugged half off. One arm free, she started unbuttoning her shirt haphazardly.

"Dear God, this is tragic," Grace said, finally swooping in to slap Caz's hands away again and finish the job.

Caz grinned at her. "You're my wife."

"I know and am already reconsidering it." Grace laughed as the last button came undone and she pushed the jacket and shirt all free.

"If you wanted...to get me naked, you only had...to ask, not...marry me." Caz laughed. Holding her left hand up to admire the plain gold band, she fell back with the support gone.

Grace shook her head. "You're going to have a big headache in the morning." Nimble fingers made light work of Caz's belt and trouser button, yanking the pants free. When she was in nothing but her underwear and socks, Grace gave up on the idea of getting her into pyjamas. "Okay, into bed."

"Was I really?" Caz asked, scooting under the covers and flopping down onto the pillow.

"Really what?" Grace asked, making her way around the bed and stripping out of her own clothes.

When no answer came, she guessed Caz was asleep again and thought nothing more of it until she slid under the duvet and Caz said quietly, "The best kiss...er you...eve...r had?"

Grace closed her eyes and remembered back to that night. There'd been too much alcohol, again, when she'd stumbled into the dark room looking for the loo and found herself in Caz's arms with no time to speak before lips were on hers and a tongue pushed into her mouth and... "Yeah," she admitted, just before the loud snore reverberated around the room.

CHAPTER EIGHT

July 2024

Men in jeans, trainers, and nothing else, moved back and forth between the van and the house, carrying boxes and furniture in before returning empty-handed to grab the next item.

They'd been a bloody godsend, Caz thought, picking up all of her stuff that morning before driving over to Grace's flat and loading up her things, and now, in the blistering, early summer heat, they were shirts-off and flying back and forth from the van to the house, unloading it all.

Another thirty minutes and they'd be done.

Caz watched from the sidelines, already instructed to keep out of their way by Grace. She felt herself being watched and turned to find a small face at the window in the house next to theirs.

Blonde ringlets and a big toothless grin looked her way. She couldn't have been any older than three, Caz guessed.

She waved.

So Caz waved back, just as the kid's mother appeared and gave a shy wave herself, clearly feeling embarrassed her kid was stalking the new neighbours. Caz smiled at her, but then her attention was brought back to the van, and to Grace handing out cans of Coke and offering encouragement to the men, who clearly liked what they saw.

Frowning, Caz wandered over.

"Alright, babe, one of those for me?" Caz asked, already reaching for a can and smiling at Grace in a way that definitely registered a 'hands fucking off'. One of the men nodded and held his palms up in defeat, but gave her a 'well done, you' kind of look.

"Uh, yep, one for you too, babe," Grace said, trying not to laugh and playing along. "I'll be upstairs making the bed up."

"Great, gonna definitely need that later," Caz called after her. And just to be sure she'd been clear with the guys, she said to them, "Got lucky there, didn't I?"

They went back to the job at hand and Caz walked back to where she'd been standing, wondering why all that had pissed her off so much.

It was typical, she thought—pretty girl and they're all like dogs in heat, sniffing around to see which one could mark their territory and pee on her first. "Not on my watch, mate," she muttered to herself.

"Excuse me," came a voice from behind; female, quiet, polite. Caz turned and found the new neighbour waving shyly at her again, this time outside and just over the fence. "Hi, I just wanted to welcome you to the neighbourhood. I'm Felicity. My Husband is Jeff. He's not home yet—still at work," Felicity explained. She looked down to her left and Caz followed her gaze to where the blonde toddler waddled around her legs. "This is Gertie."

"Cool, I'm Caz and my—" she was about to say friend, but that would be very confusing, "my partner is inside. She's called Grace."

"Oh, lovely," Felicity said with a slight rise in octave, clearly not expecting lesbians on her doorstep. Caz smiled. "I've always been very supportive of the LGBT...and all the other letters." She blushed. "Sorry, I can't always remember them."

"It's fine, you don't have to. All we ask is to be treated kindly and with respect, like you would with any other neighbour. No special treatment." Caz grinned. "Unless you want to, of course. I'm always open to a bribe with cake."

Felicity laughed nervously, unsure whether Caz was being serious or not, Caz assumed.

"I'm just kidding. Seriously, we're good people and we just want to live a nice, quiet life like everyone else."

"I'm sure everybody will get along just fine. It's a nice street and everyone is friendly—the kind of place to take your parcels in, you know?"

Caz nodded. She did know. She'd had old Mrs Firth's parcel for three weeks before she found out through the grapevine, that poor old Mrs Firth had died. She still felt bad for not raising the alarm, but Mrs Firth often went away to her daughters and Caz had just assumed that was the case then, too.

"Well, that is great to hear," Caz answered, shaking her thoughts away.

One of the guys whistled at her, waved, and shouted, "All done."

She gave him the thumbs up. "I guess I'd best get on with unpacking. It was nice to meet you both."

"Yes, same." Felicity waved.

Grace flopped down onto the sofa, swung her feet up, and leaned against Caz, who's own legs were lounging, outstretched on the longer part of the L-shaped sofa.

"I'm glad we kept your sofa and not mine," she said, sliding her arm around Grace.

"Yeah, it's bigger and comfier. We should set the TV up."

"I think we should finish our tea and then go up and finish the beds so that when we can't do anything else, we can just fall into them," Caz said, her fingers subconsciously rubbing up and down Grace's forearm. "And then I'll do the TV, and if we're still awake, we can watch a film or something."

"Can you believe we own a home?" Grace asked, before adding, "Together."

"Sure beats renting those flats we had."

Grace turned slightly. "You don't have any regrets, do you?"

"Not one." Caz smiled. "I get to spend all my time with my favourite person."

"Sometimes I worry you're going to miss out on intimacy and want something different."

Caz didn't say anything.

She'd be a liar if she said she hadn't thought about it, long term. There'd been a lot of times in her life when being single had filled long periods, but someone had always come along to break the monotony and she'd enjoyed whatever sexual element had been offered.

"Only, I was thinking—"

"Can ya stop thinking about my sex life? The entire point of this is that we've made a commitment to one another and that's not going to change."

Grace turned back and settled against her again. "I just wanted to check, that's all."

Caz kissed the top of her head. "I know, and I'm grateful you care so much about the doings in my pants."

"Shut up and don't make it creepy." Grace laughed.

"It's not me that's obsessed with me getting some action." Caz squeezed her. "What about you? You not missing dating men and getting some? Those guys today were interested."

"Ha, 'til you shooed them off."

"I didn't—okay, I did...only cos it was inappropriate."

Grace craned her neck to look up at her again. "Is that the only reason?"

"No," Caz said firmly, "...we have to make sure the neighbours don't get suspicious we're not a couple like they are." She swallowed down the last of her tea. "Right—beds, then film?"

"Yeah, let's do it." Grace sat up and watched as Caz bounced up onto her feet. "We should put some pictures up too. Make it feel like ours."

"Good plan. You can do that while I figure out the TV stuff."

Caz ran off and up the stairs. At the top, she leaned over the banister. "You look tired. I can do the beds if you want. Order a pizza and put your feet up."

"I'm okay." Grace yawned. "Alright, I am tired, but I can make a bed." She grinned up at her and wearily climbed the stairs.

"It's been a long day," Caz said, pulling her close once more, and this time holding tight. Grace's arms slid around her waist.

"Are you sure you don't want the bigger room?"

"I'm sure. You've got way more stuff than me," Caz said, remembering how many cases and bags of clothes came up.

"But the baby's room is—"

"And when the time comes, I'll get up and deal with the baby. It's not all on you to parent."

Grace smiled. "I want you to have the bigger room."

Caz held her palms up. "No point arguing with you on this, is there?"

"Nope," Grace grinned, "this is why I'm marrying you and having kids and not with some dick from wherever."

"Because I just do as I am told?" Caz chuckled.

Grace hugged her. "That...and you're thoughtful, and decent, and the best partner for raising children."

"We're going to be the best parents ever."

CHAPTER NINE

June 2025

The snoring stopped at around four in the morning, when Caz rolled over onto her front and slid one leg over Grace's thighs and an arm around her waist, her face nuzzled in against Grace's arm.

Only then could Grace finally remove the pillow from over her head and get some sleep herself. Waking up several hours later, however, to find Caz's nose just inches from her own, was interesting; not unpleasant, or weird, just...normal, and that was what she noticed most about it.

Clearly, she too must have moved and rolled over in her sleep, moving towards the embrace and not away from it.

She tried to shift herself away and couldn't. Caz tightened her grip and made a noise that sounded like, "No."

Grace giggled, which only seemed to worsen the situation when blurry eyes opened slowly and another groan sounded like, "Shh...head...hurts."

"I am not surprised. I married a drunkard." Grace smiled and kissed her forehead. "We have to get up and meet my parents for breakfast."

"They do know we got married, right...and should be unavailable for at least a month while we 'enjoy' the honeymoon phase?" Caz said, her eyes now closed again.

"A month? That's all I'm getting?" Grace huffed theatrically. "I thought you lesbians were in the honeymoon phase for years," Grace teased.

"Yeah, we are...but you've not turned to the dark side, so you get the usual straight person's two weeks, but with a bonus of two more because you had the sense to at least not marry a straight person."

Caz rolled onto her back and stretched, finally freeing Grace from her hold. Slowly, her eyes opened again, followed by a yawn and another stretch.

"I need coffee." Caz groaned as she sat up. "How many tequilas did Dani buy me?"

"About ten too many." Grace laughed, sliding out from under the duvet and crossing the room to open the curtains and flick the tiny kettle on.

Caz lifted the cover and frowned. "Why am I in my underwear and you're in cute pyjamas?"

Grace gave her a stern look, with one brow raised at the stupid question, but she answered it anyway, "Because you were so out of it. The moment you landed on the bed, you were asleep. And I was not sleeping with your boots or letting that suit get ruined, so I stripped off what I could."

"Anything to get me naked again." Caz laughed, and soon regretted it as her head pounded again. "I don't suppose you have —"

Grace was already delving into her bag. Coming up with a box of ibuprofen, she threw them across the room to Caz. "Take two, then shower. That should get the blood pumping again."

Finally sitting up, Caz puffed out her cheeks. "I'm not sure blood pumping is a good idea." She gingerly pulled her hair tie free and gently ran her fingers through the knots. "What time is it?"

"Almost ten," Grace said, her back now to Caz as she ripped open packets of instant coffee, sugar, and those horrible milk portions. Nevertheless, she divided them into two cups and added the hot water, stirring vigorously. "Here, this should liven you up."

Caz took the mug and sniffed it. "Looks grim."

"I imagine that's what it will taste like too, but needs must. Caffeine will be our God today."

Sitting at the breakfast table, Grace had budged her chair up as close to Caz as she could get. Caz had her arm slung loosely around the back of Grace's chair as they acted like the perfect couple in love.

Whispering to one another, they shared light kisses on cheeks and lots of staring into each other's eyes whenever Ron or Lila was watching too intently.

The initial embarrassment when Ron had asked, "So, good night's sleep?" without thinking, had surpassed, and Grace had allowed Caz to make a witty comment back. Her dad's cheeks had gone bright beetroot as soon as he'd realised what he'd asked, but he got over it.

"It don't feel right, you not having a honeymoon," Lila said, when coffee had arrived and Ron was eyeing up the breakfast buffet.

They'd talked about the honeymoon at length, and though they'd both agreed a break would be nice, they also knew how much having a baby was going to cost and decided it was money they didn't want to waste.

"We've got other stuff we want to get done," Grace said. They hadn't mentioned to anyone else about starting a family. They'd both decided there was no point until there was something to tell them.

"Like what? The house is immaculate," Ron chipped in,

having spent most weekends round there, painting walls and hanging paper.

They'd had to move all of Grace's stuff into Caz's room for the duration of the upstairs getting decorated. And then they'd moved it all into Grace's room while Caz's room was done, with Caz having to get up early and make sure her bed was made before Ron and the boys got there. Then they had to move all of Caz's stuff back when it was all finally finished.

"We're thinking about a hot tub in the garden," Caz said as nonchalantly as you like, while stifling a yawn when she felt Grace stiffen.

Lila's face lit up. "Oh, that would be nice... Can just see you two frolicking in there." She winked.

Grace blushed, but said nothing when Caz took her hand, raised it, and kissed it. "Yeah, that's what we thought."

"Honeymoon phase." Grace smiled.

Ron's face edged towards beetroot again. "On that note, I'll get some breakfast. Caz?"

"Hm?" Caz said, tearing her eyes away from mooning over Grace. "Oh, breakfast? Yes, starving, shall I get you something too, babe?"

Grace grinned at the nickname that was becoming quite regularly used lately.

"Would you?" she said in her most demure way, eyelashes batting for good effect.

"Of course, darling, anything for my wife." Caz waggled her brows. "The full works, or starting with the pastries and making your way around?"

"Hm...choices. Surprise me."

She continued watching as Caz and her father walked away, happily chatting.

"Can't keep your eyes off her, can you?" Her mum smiled when Grace turned quickly. "It's alright, you're allowed to ogle. She's your gorgeous wife."

"Yes." She turned back to look at Caz once more. "She is."

CHAPTER TEN

August 2024

"I still can't believe you're getting married," Dani said. She was leaning on the wing and staring down through the engine at Caz.

"Well, I can't believe I got you a job here and you haven't fucked it up, but we live and learn," Caz said sarcastically, but with a grin on her face.

"I know." Dani grinned back. "But...still—you, married...I just can't imagine it."

"Why not?" Caz asked. "Pass the ten, will you."

Dani leaned across to the toolbox and found the relevant wrench. "This one?"

Caz peered up. "Yep." She squeezed her fingers through the gap and caught it when Dani dropped it.

"Because...it's Grace."

"What's that supposed to mean?"

"She's like the straightest person I've ever met," Dani laughed, "and she fancies you? Even after knowing you all these years?"

Caz rolled out until her head and shoulders were clear and she could properly frown at Dani. "Sometimes people just love each other; nothing to do with labels or sexuality. And anyway, maybe Grace is pansexual and my being a woman doesn't make any difference."

"But she's never dated a woman before, has she?"

"Does it matter? Is there a time limit on when anyone can do something by?" Caz grabbed a screwdriver and pushed herself back under. "Anyway, she's been dating me, as you well know."

Dani shrugged. "I'm just curious...what's she like?"

"What do you mean, 'what's she like'? You've met her."

Leaning as close to the engine as she could, Dani whispered, "In bed."

"None of your fucking business, Dani. What the fuck kind of question is that?" Caz rolled out from the car completely and jumped to her feet, dropping the wrench with a clang to the floor.

Frank turned. So did Rob and Kev, but nobody moved except for Dani, who flinched backward a step.

"Look, I'm sorry, alright...I was just curious." She held her hands up, aware she'd pushed too far. "Caz, I'm sorry, you're right."

"Totally out of fucking order, am I clear?" Caz's face went red. She'd rarely gotten this angry, unless it came to Grace. "I love her. I'm marrying her, and I don't care if nobody here understands, or thinks she's not gay enough." She glanced around at all the eyes on her and watched as, one by one, they all looked away.

"I got it." Dani took another step back. "I swear, not another word. I believe you."

"Fuck's sake, we've been together for months and *now* you say you believe me?"

Dani held her finger up. "That didn't sound how it sounded in my head and wasn't what I meant. I just...we're all surprised, that's all."

"What the bleeding hell is going on out here? I'm trying

to speak to a customer and all I can hear is a racket." Ron looked back and forth between the pair of them.

"Nothing, boss, I just dropped a tool," Caz said, bending to pick it up.

"Yeah, and we got a bit rowdy, you know, woohoo," Dani offered.

He wasn't buying it but nodded anyway. "Well, keep it down."

They watched him walk away.

"Stop being surprised and just accept it," Caz said quietly, "because it's not going to change. We are getting married and she's my person, alright?"

"Yes. I'm sorry."

"Right, then we'll say no more." Caz wiped her hands on her vest and stuck out a palm. "Shake on it."

Dani eyed the greasy palm and pulled a face. "Really?"

"Want me to spit on it too?"

"Nope," Dani said quickly, and thrust her hand out, shaking Caz's hand. "Friends again?"

Caz grinned. "Always."

When Grace got home and poked her head around the living room door, she found Caz with her feet up on the couch, bottle of beer in hand and the TV on a game show, looking like the world had caved in. She took a step back into the lounge and prepared for whatever might come.

"Hey, I'm home," she called out, and then went with a low-end, small-talk comment to test the waters. "God, it's so hot out still."

Caz didn't answer.

"Hey," Grace repeated, coming into the room, "I said it's still so hot out."

"Yeah, scorcher," Caz said absently, not looking at her. She swigged her beer and started flicking through the channels.

"What's up?" Grace asked, perching herself on the arm of the sofa.

Caz shrugged. "Had a row with Dani today and it just got me thinking…"

Grace waited a moment to see if the thinking developed into words, but it didn't and the silence continued. She slid down onto the cushions.

"So, what did you row about?" she probed gently.

Now Caz turned to face her. "Us." She shrugged again. "Apparently she didn't believe we were a real couple, or that you were suddenly gay, or that…" She looked away, her cheeks flushing.

"That?" Grace asked.

Caz huffed. "She had the nerve to ask me what you were like in bed."

Grace snorted. "Oh, and you said?"

"I said for her to mind her own business, that's what I said, then I got mad and we had a bit of a row." She pursed her lips and narrowed her eyes. "Well, I said a lot of stuff and she backed down, but you get it, right?"

"You defended my honour like any good girlfriend would. Yes, I get it." Grace smiled at her. "So, did she accept that?"

Caz nodded. "Yeah."

"Okay, then."

"But…if Dani doesn't believe us, then what about everyone else?"

Repositioning herself so she was now sitting beside Caz, Grace said, "Does it matter? We're getting married next year, and we will have a baby. We already own a house together. Who cares if one person is questioning if it's real or not?"

"I guess. I just don't like it that… What if they're talking about us?"

"Again, does it matter?" She reached for Caz's hand. "You love me, right?"

Caz nodded. "I do, yeah."

"Right, and I love you. And just because how we choose to show and share that love isn't the way society or our friends and family might expect, doesn't change it."

Caz smiled and offered her the bottle, which she took.

"You're right." Caz nodded. "I just got caught off guard. I didn't think people would be expecting proof that we—"

"We can give them proof, if you want." Grace swigged from the bottle.

"And how would we do that?" Caz laughed, accepting the bottle back.

Grace shrugged. "I don't know. You could kiss me in full view of a few of them? Or… Oh, I know, we could stage some photos?"

"Stage photos?"

"Yeah, like…you've taken pics of girlfriends, right? When you're all snuggled up in bed and they look all cute sleeping on you?"

Caz thought about it. "Yeah, maybe when I was younger. Would be a bit creepy now."

Grace laughed. "Why?"

"Consent, init."

Grace smiled. The idea of kissing hadn't been turned down, but a staged photo pretending to be asleep was. "Alright, well, we can stage pics where I am awake. But under a duvet, naked shoulders, cuddling, looking at each other…candid stuff." She shrugged. "And then you can show people how adorable we are together."

"It wouldn't hurt to have something like that…I mean, we should, shouldn't we?"

Grace nodded. She thought back to all the mornings they had woken up like that. Not naked, but snuggled up on a sofa, in a bed, the back of a car, or a tent. Their entire relationship had been filled with moments most people would have assumed meant they were a couple, but then, most people didn't see those times and they'd never thought to take photos. "Yes, we should."

A phone beeped and Grace sat up properly to see which of them was being bothered. It was her own phone that lit up. She read the screen, then frowned, her mouth scrunched and moved side to side in the way it did when she wasn't pleased.

"What's up?" Caz asked, slightly concerned.

"Your day's about to get worse." Grace grimaced, "Mum and Dad are on their way over."

"Alright, that's not—"

"They want to stay the night."

"Oh."

Caz was like a whippet—up off the couch and heading up the stairs as fast as her feet would carry her.

"We'll have to move your stuff into mine," she shouted down at Grace, who was wearily making her way up the stairs. "It would make sense we'd share the bigger room, right?"

"Yeah, I guess so," Grace said when she'd gotten to the top. She stood on the top step, out of the way, as Caz whizzed past carrying armfuls of her clothes, still on hangers.

"Don't just stand there, Grace," Caz urged. "How long will they be?"

Grace glanced at her watch, "They said they'd pick up an Indian take-away as a thank you and then head straight over. We've probably got an hour."

"Alright, doable," Caz said, running past her again.

"Caz?"

She slid to a halt and turned. "Yes, Grace?"

"We don't have to move everything. We can just say I have so many clothes that we use the spare wardrobes."

"That makes sense." Caz pointed a finger at her like a gun.

"I know...all we need to do is move my day-to-day stuff, the nightstand stuff, and..." She shook her head. "Definitely anything in the top drawer of my bedside cabinet."

Caz nodded. "Okay, I'll do that—"

"Oh, no you won't," Grace said, budging her out of the way to get past. "That is out of bounds."

It took a minute and then Caz grinned. "Oh, the battery powered bestie is in there."

Grace ignored her.

"What other little delights do you have in there, Grace?" Caz teased, launching herself onto Grace's bed. She lay on her side, leaning on one elbow as she watched Grace go bright red.

"Nothing to concern you, nosy parker. And for your

information, nothing in there is battery operated."

"Are you running your orgasms off the national grid?" Caz burst into laughter. "No wonder the smart meter is always flashing red."

"You think you're so funny, don't you?" Grace said, but she couldn't hold back the laughter either. "Will you sod off so I can pack my stuff? It's bad enough I'm going to have to kip in with you tonight."

"Don't pretend you're not excited about it. It will be like camping out. An adventure!"

The doorbell rang.

"What the heck?" Caz said, jumping to her feet and standing up. She looked at her watch. An hour hadn't passed. "That can't be them already?"

Grace looked panicked. "Well, if it is, stall them." She reached under her bed and pulled out a small travel case. "Go," she urged, as Caz lingered.

The doorbell rang again, and this time Caz raced onto the landing and down the stairs, yanking the door open and forcing a grin onto her face.

"Hey," she said, gawking at Lila and Ron and then at the suitcase that looked like they were planning to stay for a week, but seeing no take-away. "Come in." She reached for the case, but Ron had hold of it.

"No need," he said, and lifted it over the threshold once Lila had stepped inside and kissed Caz on the cheek.

"Where's Grace?" she asked.

Caz turned towards the stairs and said loudly enough, "She's just getting changed—long day at work."

"Bloody workmen down the road hit a water mains. The entire street is without water for the foreseeable," Ron explained while he pulled his jacket off. "Can't even flush the loo." He shook his head.

"And I said it's fine, Grace and Caz won't mind us crashing." Lila smiled before heading off to the kitchen. "Dinner will be here soon. Shall I get the plates out?"

Caz looked to Ron, who rolled his eyes. "It was busy in the restaurant, so we said a delivery would probably be just as fast."

"Right, cool," Caz answered. "Must admit, I am famished."

"Good, cos Lila ordered enough to feed the entire garage." He glanced up and grinned at the sight of Grace serenely coming down the stairs. "Hello, Sweetpea."

"Hey, Dad," Grace said, sidling up to Caz, who instinctively put her arm around Grace's shoulders and pulled her close.

"They've got no water...for the foreseeable future," Caz said, kissing the side of Grace's head for good effect.

"Well, let's hope it's not as bad as that, eh?" Ron said. "I like me own bed."

"Me too," Caz whispered. Grace grinned but poked her for good measure.

"Night, then," Grace said from the landing as her parents went to bed in her room. She carried two glasses of water and nudged the door to Caz's room open with her hip.

"Alright?" Caz said, sitting up in bed, wearing a pair of pyjamas Grace knew she wouldn't usually be wearing.

"Yes." She passed a glass to Caz. "Are you going to be comfortable sleeping in PJs?"

"Probably not," Caz sighed, "but preferable to meeting Ron

on the landing in the middle of the night in my vest and pants… so…"

"You have an ensuite," Grace said, glancing towards the small bathroom.

"But I might need to get up and get a drink or—"

Grace held up the glass of water in her hand. "How thirsty will you get? Do you need to be checked for diabetes?"

"Fine. I didn't want to make things awkward for you, that's all."

"I've seen you in your vest and pants a million times." Grace laughed. "Get them off and go to sleep."

Huffing, Caz reached under the covers and acrobatically removed her pyjama bottoms and then she unbuttoned the top.

"Oh, for God's sake, you had your vest and pants on underneath?"

"I came prepared." Caz grinned.

"For what? Me trying to strip you in my sleep?" Grace stared at her and laughed. "You're an idiot."

"I'm *your* idiot." Caz reached out and flicked the light switch off. "Night, Grace."

CHAPTER ELEVEN

June 2025

"Maybe we should have had a honeymoon," Caz said as she folded her clothes and packed them into the joint suitcase, their dresses and suits already hanging in bags to protect them. From what, she didn't know. It wasn't like they'd be wearing them again, was it?

"You said a hot tub was more fun," Grace replied. She glanced at Caz through the mirror.

"Yeah, and you can't deny it isn't." Caz grinned, knowing full well, in this heat, Grace was going straight in it when they got back.

Applying lipstick, Grace continued to watch Caz through the mirror as she dropped the last item into the case and then sat on the bed.

"Did you want a holiday?"

Grace finished dabbing her lips with a tissue and turned to face her.

"I would like a holiday, yes."

"Why didn't you say that when we were discussing the honeymoon and the hot tub?"

Shrugging, Grace turned back to the mirror and spoke to Caz through it once more.

"Because you were so excited about the hot tub and I wanted that for you."

Sighing, Caz stood up. It took two steps before she came up behind Grace and placed her hands on each shoulder. Squeezing gently as she bent, and with their heads side by side, their eyes locked in the mirror, she said, "In future, can you remember that maybe, I'd like your happiness to come first, too, and we can always find a compromise to do both things?"

Grace reached up, stroking her face.

"You're right, I shouldn't decide for you what you want."

Caz turned slightly and placed a gentle kiss to Grace's cheek.

"I'm going to book us a holiday. We have the rest of this week off to do something."

Grace smiled. "Nothing too expensive."

"Don't worry, I'll find us a deal." She was already reaching for her phone to start the search. "Anywhere in particular you fancy?"

"No—" she frowned, "actually, I mean...I've never had to consider it before but...somewhere safe? I know we're not technically a gay couple, but to the outside world that's what we are and—"

"I get it." Caz smiled sadly. It was an unfortunate part of this process—others judged. "Most of Europe is fine... What about Portugal?"

"That could work. I've never been. It might be nice to see somewhere new." Collecting her make-up and gently putting it all back into the bag that carried it, she peeked back at Caz again. "And then I thought we could..."

Caz stopped what she was doing and gave her all the attention, not interrupting.

"I thought maybe we could think about the baby again?"

CHAPTER TWELVE

December 2024

"Right, where do you want to put it?" Caz asked, dragging the seven-foot monster of a tree through the door as Grace wandered in behind, carrying bags full of decorations.

"I was thinking if we push the sofa down, it could go in that corner." Grace pointed to the spot.

"Okie dokie," Caz answered, lifting and twisting until she could squeeze the fir through the doorway and drop it gently to the floor.

She didn't wait, getting herself wedged into the space between the wall and the sofa, using her thighs for leverage, and pushed until it moved as far as it would go.

"I can help," Grace said.

"No, you can put your feet up. We haven't spent all this time finding the best donor and paying a fancy clinic to impregnate you, for you to be shifting furniture." She took Grace's hand and led her over to the sofa. "Sit, feet up, I'll get you a nice hot chocolate made. How does that sound?"

"Sound's perfect. And you're right. I know we don't even know yet if it's worked, but I do need to remember to not…" Her words drifted away. It was difficult not knowing one way or the other and they still had almost a week to go before she could do a test to see if it worked. "It might not have worked anyway."

"It's going to work," Caz said emphatically.

Grace nodded. "If it doesn't—"

"It will," Caz repeated, sitting down beside her. "And if it doesn't, then we'll try again. Try not to think about it."

Grace's laugh had an edge of sarcasm to it. "I potentially have another human growing in me, that's hard not to think about."

"I know. It's all kind of crazy, isn't it? Just a couple of months have passed and now we might have—" Her hand tentatively reached to touch Grace's tummy and then stopped, hovering above it, unsure.

Grace took her hand and pulled it down until Caz's palm flattened out over her bellybutton. "You can touch."

"Have you thought about whether you'd want a boy or a girl?"

Grace shook her head. "I don't mind."

"Me either. Mind, I mean. I thought about it and came up with positives and negatives to both, so figured whatever it was, it's going to be fun...and trouble."

Curling into Caz's side, Grace chuckled.

"It will have you for a parent—of course it's going to be trouble."

"It *will* know how to change a tyre."

Grace pinched her playfully. "Hey, you said to call you whenever there was a problem with the car." Still chuckling, she said, "They will know how to protect those they love, and how to fight their own battles, and what love looks like."

"Yeah." Caz sighed. "What are they going to get from you?"

Pinching her again, Grace laughed. "You're horrible."

The week passed in a blur. So much needed to be done to get ready for Christmas, which was fast upon them. Work was manic for Caz, with people wanting their cars checked over, or tyres changed in preparation for long drives to see family or go away for the holidays.

Not that she complained; the overtime meant she could buy things for the nursery and get Grace something extra for Christmas. Afterall, wasn't Grace giving her the biggest gift any human could give another?

It would be their first, and probably their last, opportunity to spend Christmas together, just the two of them, before their family blossomed.

With Ron and Lila heading to Grace's brother's family for Christmas in Norfolk, and Caz not having any family to worry about, it was an easy decision to stay home. They hadn't told anyone about the potential family addition yet, either, so Caz was going all out to make it the best.

Fatigued, she staggered in through the front door, already pulling her jacket off wearily and ready to kick her boots into the cupboard under the stairs.

Exhaustion had hit two hours ago.

"I'm home," she called out. Finally, pushing the second boot from her foot, she ran her hands through her hair and caught herself in the hall mirror. "Attractive, Caz." She yawned and tried to wipe the smear of oil that had managed to evade her quick face wash before she'd left the garage. "Grace?"

Checking her watch, it was gone eight. Grace didn't have any plans this evening that Caz could remember. Wandering into the kitchen, the lights were off and nothing was cooking. She frowned. Caz crossed the room to the calendar on the wall and checked to see if Grace had any appointments she'd forgotten about, but there were none.

"Grace?" she tried again, and walked through the dining room and into the lounge.

No sign.

A surge of panic began to rise, adrenaline coursing and winding its way into her system. She should be home from work by now.

Back in the hallway, she listened for signs telling her anyone was home and heard nothing, just sounds from cars and people passing by outside. She looked outside; Grace's car was definitely on the drive.

And then she stopped.

She cocked her head to listen better. There had definitely been something she couldn't quite put her finger on—noise within the house.

It happened again; a small whimper.

Bounding up two stairs at a time, Caz reached the landing in seconds and listened again. Her bedroom door was open, so was the bathroom, but Grace's door was firmly closed.

She tapped lightly on it. "Grace? Can I come in?"

This time, the whimper became a sob and Caz forgot politeness and opened the door. Peering into the darkness, she could just make out the figure of Grace, curled up on her bed.

"Grace? What's wrong?"

She edged nearer, until she could slide onto the bed and push herself closer. Just as she reached out, Grace turned and burrowed into her, sobbing uncontrollably.

She didn't need to be told; she felt it. Her arms slid around Grace easily and she pulled her closer. The pain, the heartbreak—all of it trembling within her embrace.

They'd suffer together.

"I'm sorry…"

"It's okay," she whispered, and kissed her head over and over until even she believed it might be okay.

Christmas morning was cold. The kind of cold where, without central heating, you would stay in bed under the duvet and fester until you were so hungry you had no choice but to get up.

Snow had been falling for over a week now and the entire area was blanketed. On any other day, Caz would have found some joy in waking up to a white Christmas, but what was there to be joyous about?

They'd gone out the night before and met friends at the bar. Keeping everything pushed down and unspoken in an attempt to not upset Grace, Caz had allowed herself to be dragged along. They tried to appear like everything was rosy because they hadn't told anyone about the pregnancy, or the fact that it hadn't worked.

"What was the point?" Grace had said.

Tons of people were there, all having fun until the snow started up again and everyone left to get home safely. How they'd both put on smiles and happy voices, she didn't know, but then, they were good at lying to people now, weren't they?

Maybe even to themselves.

Grace had cried the moment the key was in the door. She'd cried every night. Caz could hear her sobs. Every time, she'd get up, pad barefoot across the landing and knock gently on the door, then she'd climb into bed and wrap Grace in her arms, and they'd stay like that 'til morning.

It broke her heart.

Each morning, Grace would get up, put her face on, dress silently, and go to work with a packed lunch Caz had made the night before.

She moved through the motions until she could come home and climb back into bed again.

Lunch remained barely touched.

Caz had knocked the extra hours at work on the head, wanting to be at home with Grace. Of course, everyone had had a good giggle at that.

The love birds all alone for Christmas.

It had been the garage joke: How much Caz was doting on Grace. They'll be married soon, they'd all say. Caz would laugh it all off before she'd pack up and head home for another night of being useless.

Getting home, she'd find Grace already in bed, curled up, sometimes crying, other times just lying there and staring off into space.

That was how she had found Grace Christmas morning, but something shifted in Caz. There was supportive, and then there was permissive.

Allowing this to continue was hurting them both, wasn't it?

Caz got up, showered and dressed, before heading downstairs to make Grace a breakfast she didn't expect she would eat but was getting anyway. Life had to move on, otherwise they would stagnate.

A toasted English muffin, halved and shared between two plates, one poached egg on each half, a generous pouring of hollandaise sauce, and a sprinkling of rocket. She placed one plate onto the tray along with cutlery, a glass of orange juice, and a small present, wrapped perfectly.

Balanced on her palm, she knocked gently and didn't bother to wait for Grace to answer, because there rarely was one.

"Morning, I got you some breakfast," she said as cheerily as she could manage. Grace didn't move. "Merry Christmas."

Caz put the tray down onto the bedside cabinet and walked around the room to the window, drawing the curtains open. "Still snowing," she said, trying to keep her voice happy and not break down herself.

"Sweetheart?" Caz came around to the side of the bed where Grace was facing and crouched down. "I think it's time to get up, don't you?"

Grace mumbled something Caz couldn't hear. It didn't matter. Caz made a decision, Grace needed a wake-up call, and a shower. She stood up and left the room, coming back a moment later to find Grace still hiding under the covers.

"Grace, I love you, and I know you're hurting, but this can't go on. We've still got options." She waited a second, and when no movement came, she yanked the cover back and slid her arm under Grace, lifting her up before she had any chance to even consider what was happening.

Her eyes wide and angry, hair sticking up, Grace finally spoke. "Put me down." She looked like a scarecrow.

"I'm not putting you down. I will not allow you to continue this."

"I just want to be left alone."

"And I want my best friend to return to the world and spend Christmas with me." Caz twisted around and carried her out into the hallway, kicking the bathroom door open with her foot. "You need a shower."

Steam billowed in the small room from where Caz had switched the shower on in preparation.

Grace glared at her. "Put me down." She punched Caz on the arm. Not hard enough to bruise, but hard enough to make a point. But the point was lost amongst the tears. And out of nowhere, she stopped fighting and clung onto Caz, unwilling to let go.

"It's time to come back to me," Caz said, stepping into the shower. The water hit and soaked through her shirt and jeans.

The pair of them just stood there, dripping wet.

And finally, the sobbing quieted, the fingers released their grip, and Caz let Grace's feet land on the floor, unmoving, as Caz, eyes closed, removed Grace's pyjamas, turned her around, and washed her. She rubbed shampoo into her hair and took care of her in the only way she knew how, passing her a sponge for those more intimate areas.

Finished, Caz switched the water off and reached for a towel, wrapping Grace in it before she stripped out of her own clothes and found a second towel.

"We have too much to live for, and too many dreams to create," she said, and then it happened: Grace nodded.

"I'm sorry…"

"For what?"

Her eyes wet as she said, "That I couldn't look after our baby."

"That's not what happened. It was too soon," Caz said gently. "Most likely you weren't pregnant."

"Doesn't matter. I couldn't—"

"No," Caz said, placing a finger against her lips. "There's no blame, there's no shame. It didn't work, that's all. There's nothing wrong with you. You just had a period like every other month, that's all."

Grace nodded, her grip tightening on Caz.

"We're going to get through this, and if you want to try again, we'll talk about it, but right now...I need you." Caz wiped the tears away on her own cheeks, but it didn't stop them flowing.

"Okay." Grace reached up and cupped Caz's cheek. "Okay."

CHAPTER THIRTEEN

June 2025

Getting home, the house felt quiet. They'd only been away three days for the wedding, and yet, it felt like a lifetime since they'd just chilled and vegged out on their own furniture.

"Right, cup of tea? And then I'll run down to the chippy and get—"

"Sit," Grace said, patting the space on the sofa next to her. "I want to talk."

Caz chewed the inside of her mouth before nodding and finally sitting down. "Okay." Both feet were planted firmly on the ground, legs apart, elbows resting on them with her hands clasped tightly together.

"Can you look at me, please?" Grace asked gently, aware this wasn't the easiest of conversations. When Caz took a deep breath and exhaled slowly, but sat back and turned to face her, Grace smiled. "I know it's hard, and last time was...upsetting."

"Heartbreaking...watching you cry like that, it—" She breathed deeply again and stared up at the ceiling.

"I know." Grace touched her arm and got her attention once more. "I know, and I hate that we were both so disappointed. But I want to try again. And I know it's expensive —"

"It's not the money," Caz said quietly.

Grace sighed. "Have you changed your mind?"

"No." Caz shook her head. "No, I haven't. I want a family

with you. I just…if it doesn't work again, then what?"

"I don't know, try again?"

"How long do we keep trying? How many heartbreaks can you take—can I watch?" Caz took her hand. "Last time, we were so caught up in the excitement of the potential, that we didn't think about the reality of failing and now we know, now we can't ignore that, so this time we need to be more prepared for all outcomes."

Grace nodded. "I agree. It's been over six months, and I think, with the wedding and everything all so perfect between us, I'm ready. We said we'd talk about it again after the wedding, but if I'm honest, I've been ready to talk about it for weeks."

"Alright," Caz said, and couldn't not smile when Grace's face lit up. "Compromise: We speak to the doctor and book the procedure, and then we go on holiday and forget all about it for a week. And when we get back, if you're still adamant you want to do it, we'll do it."

Grace shook her head. "I want to do it. I'm adamant now, but—"

"It's not that simple, though, is it?"

"No, we'd need to find another donor."

Caz nodded. "Yes, and this time we have to be realistic."

"Geriatric eggs," Grace mumbled. That was what they'd been told by the clinic: A lower chance of pregnancy due to Grace's age.

They'd left that meeting feeling insulted. They weren't that old and already had geriatric labels.

Caz smiled sadly. "Thirty percent success rate felt bigger then."

"One in three chance. I think it's worth it."

"I just…" Sliding to her knees on the floor, Caz held Grace's hand more tightly. "I worry what might happen to you if it fails. I want…I want you to be happy, and I want…I want this to be everything we want it to be, but if it doesn't work, I need to know you're going to be okay."

"I'll be alright." Grace touched her face. "I want to do this. It's why we got married."

"I know."

"And I don't want to use the clinic again." She smiled at Caz's confused face. "Hear me out. I found a website that explains it all. You get the donor, and you have them checked out, and then you can arrange to do it yourself at home."

"But—"

"I just want to be at my most relaxed. And I wasn't relaxed at the clinic. It was all so sterile and I had this stranger between my legs, and I'd just like it to be more natural next time. Millions of women get pregnant every day, and I just…maybe the donation being frozen was part of the issue and we just need something…fresher. "

Caz grimaced at that. "Right, so we find a donor, they come over, and then you'd just do it yourself with a turkey baster?"

Grace laughed. "No, we'd get a donor, get him checked out at the clinic still—I'm not avoiding that part—and then we either have him come over or meet in a hotel. He does the business and then…you'd do it."

Caz almost fainted. "You what?"

"Which part are you having trouble with?" Grace asked, chuckling still.

Standing up, Caz rubbed her arms, a sudden chill in the air sending goosebumps all over her body.

"All of it, but mostly the last part."

"Caz, don't you want to be part of the process?"

Caz turned away quickly, moving towards the wood burner and the opportunity to do something that would keep her hands busy, before she stopped and turned back to face Grace.

"I assumed coming into the room and holding your hand again was me being part of the process. I can't put...in your..." She used her hands to make movements that had nothing to do with anything.

"Vagina?"

"Yes, that. I can't be—" She grabbed a log and opened the door to the wood burner.

"Oh, for goodness' sake. You're a lesbian, you've seen dozens. Mine's no different." Grace laughed.

"Are you mad? Of course yours is different." She dropped the log and picked up the brush and began clearing out the ash from the last time they'd lit it, which was weeks ago.

"You've seen me naked loads of times."

"Getting changed! You taking your clothes off in the same room isn't the same as me staring straight at your cooch, and then...then having to physically go where no girl has gone before."

Grace laughed. "You're an idiot."

"I'm *your* idiot," Caz reminded her.

"Yes, mine. We're a married couple. You have every right to be staring into my *cooch* for these purposes."

Caz put her fingers in her ears. "La la la la la." And left the room.

"Caroline! Where are you going?"

"Out and away from anything that makes me think about

looking at your—"

"Fine, but get your head around it. I'll start packing for this trip."

It took twenty minutes for Caz to walk down to the river complex and cross the bridge into Bath Street. She liked it down here, this small area being a crossroads of sorts.

She and Grace lived in Banbury Hollow, which was one point that gathered at the river. Next to them was the town of Woodington on one side, Bath Street on the other, with another village, Amberfield, directly opposite on the map. But it was right here that they all congregated like a mothers' meeting for lesbians and the artsy crowd, or those just wanting to relax somewhere quiet at one of the numerous eateries and bars that lined both sides of the river.

It was a vibrant and busy place all year round, and because of the bar, it was known for being the gay parade. She could recognise a lot of faces from the bar as she walked along the embankment towards Blanca's. But her mind wasn't on registering any smiles or hellos. All she could think about was Grace's latest request because it had triggered something she hadn't sensed was there before.

She was horny.

This past year had been amazing, more than she could ever have dreamed it would be, and Grace had been right, they were intimate with one another and the perfect partners in many ways.

They watched TV snuggled on the sofa. They comforted one another when one was upset. They held hands as they talked their frustrations through. There were kisses, nothing sexual, but always a kiss goodbye, a kiss hello, a thank you kiss, a 'you're adorable' head kiss. In fact, they kissed all the time, didn't they?

But never like lovers.

And in that entire time, Caz hadn't thought about anything further. She'd sorted herself out when the need arose, just like she'd done for any other period of time she didn't have a sexual partner.

Sex had never been the be-all and end-all for Caz. Chemistry and emotions were very much needed before she got excited about sex with anyone.

Other people's sex parts were something special, not to be gawped at, or touched without the other ingredients that would create a distinctly different moment.

The problem, though, now that she thought about it, was that they had emotional connection and chemistry, and Grace was special. And they were married.

This was a major head fuck.

One she hadn't expected she'd need to deal with. There had never been any expectation she'd ever become *that* intimate with Grace, despite her wife's jokey offers.

Impregnating your wife felt pretty intimate in the grand scheme of things. Possibly the most intimate she could ever consider being with anyone.

She pushed the door open to the bar and stepped inside. It was busy. People were enjoying their last moments of the weekend. She paused in the doorway. *What if Dani and the gang were here?* They'd question why she was here, and not at home with her new wife.

Backing out, she quickly turned and walked towards the bridge again and into Amberfield. There was a coffee shop she liked that would still be open, just about.

Questions and thoughts fired off in her mind again. It wasn't right, was it? To be gawping at your best friend's vagina? But it's scientific, she corrected herself. Gawping suggests leering, and she'd not be doing that; she'd be making a baby.

She thought back to their previous attempt. It had all been so simple. They went to the clinic, did all the tests, and picked a donor. Then they'd gone back to the clinic, Grace had had the procedure, and they went home and waited.

And then the heartbreak.

Maybe Grace was right. Maybe something more natural was the way forward. And didn't she want to give Grace everything she wanted? Didn't she want to make her happy?

CHAPTER FOURTEEN

She got home and kicked off her boots, reaching down to straighten them up and make sure there wasn't any mud on the floor. With that sorted, she took off her coat and hung it up. Turning, she found Grace standing in the doorway to the living room, arms folded, leaning against the jamb, one brow raised and a curious smile on her face.

"Well?" she said, and Caz realised, yet again, just how much this woman understood her, allowing the space to process and not pester her for answers until the time was right.

"Okay, I'll do it. But…" Caz held up a finger. "I can't be down there like a doctor, fiddling around."

Grace frowned a little, a questioning narrowing of the eyes. "Okay, what is your compromise?"

Caz walked down the hallway to the kitchen with Grace following. "I was thinking, I could lie beside you and reach down, but be focusing on your face."

"Alright, and how would you know if you've hit the spot, so to speak?"

Rolling her eyes, Caz huffed. "I know where the spot is. And anyway, you can tell me."

Grace smiled. "Thank you."

Flicking the kettle on, Caz returned the smile.

"But first, we're going to get away for a few days. Sod Portugal, let's stay local and not waste time travelling."

Closing the space between them, Grace flung her arms around Caz's waist as Caz dropped teabags into mugs. "I can definitely agree to that. Anywhere in mind?"

"Well, I saw someone post a video about West Wittering. It's not that far—sandy beaches for miles. Kate Winslet lives there."

"Oh, well, if it's good enough for Kate…" Grace grinned, finally letting go of Caz. She moved to the side and leaned back against the worktop. "It is the weather for the beach, and no point going abroad when you've got it almost on the doorstep."

"Yep. So, I thought we'd have a cup of tea and then get on Airbnb and find something for tomorrow?"

"I would love that," Grace said, straightening up to kiss Caz's cheek. "You're too good to me."

"Uh, I think you'll find, I'm just treating you how you deserve to be treated."

Grace was quiet for a moment, before she said, "Yes. You are." And then she left the room.

Shrugging, Caz finished the tea-making and then followed to find Grace sitting cross-legged on the sofa with a magazine in her lap.

"Here you go." Caz placed the mugs down onto the coffee table and then threw herself into the corner of the couch and pulled her feet up. With her phone already in her hand, she started scrolling on the Airbnb app.

"Just so you know," Grace said, as Caz continued to scroll. "I'm really happy with you."

Caz looked up and found the eyes of her wife set on her with such an intensity, that for a moment, she forgot this was her best friend and not a lover.

She shook herself out of it, scolding herself for even contemplating Grace as anything more. That was not the deal they'd agreed on.

"I'm happy you're happy," Caz finally responded. She bit her lip hard when a jolt of something sexually exciting hit right between her legs. "I'm just going to—" She jumped up, phone dropping on the couch. "Loo. I need the loo."

"Alright," Grace said, reaching for her tea.

Caz moved quickly.

Into the hall and up the stairs two at a time, she bounded into the bathroom and locked the door behind her.

"No, no, no, no, no," she said quickly to herself. Her hand moved into her hair, fingers gripping her scalp. "This is not happening."

Her clit throbbed a response that said otherwise.

Squeezing her thighs together just made it worse, and when her eyes closed, all she saw was the image of Grace smiling at her.

Twisting the tap to cold, she thrust her hands under the flow of the water and splashed her face with the icy blast.

"You can't suddenly have romantic feelings for your wife," she muttered, staring at herself in the mirror. And then she laughed at how ridiculous that would sound to anyone listening. "Okay, get a grip. It's just because you're missing sexy times right now, and she's…she's down there being her usual cute, gorgeous self, and that's getting all twisted up in your head."

Her clit throbbed again, and she thrust her hands back under the water and repeated the process.

As she stared back in the mirror, she realised something: Being married to your best friend wasn't going to be as easy as she'd thought it would be.

CHAPTER FIFTEEN

The beach stretched for what looked like miles of golden sand with water lapping at the shoreline. Boats in the distance bobbed about in the channel between the mainland and the Isle of Wight.

Grace had picked the spot and laid out their towels, while Caz had banged in the sticks that would hold the windbreaker in place. Not that it was particularly windy, but it did offer an element of privacy.

She'd laughed when Grace had returned from the shop with a small open-faced tent, but now, with it all set up and their things safely stored inside and away from the sand that would inevitably get into every crevice, Caz had to admit it was a spark of genius.

"You can get changed in there, without everyone staring," Grace had stated when Caz had finished putting it together. "And we won't get sand in the sandwiches." Caz chuckled at that.

When everything was arranged just how Grace wanted it, Caz pulled off her vest and dropped her shorts. She already had her bikini on underneath and had slathered herself in sun lotion before they'd left, preferring to give it time to soak in and not have to give her skin a vigorous rub with the sand sticking to her.

She dropped down to her towel and stretched out, adjusting her sunglasses to block out the glare of the afternoon sunshine.

"This is the life," she said, looking up at Grace, who was still admiring the view out to sea.

Grace turned and peered down at her. "Isn't it just. And

really, it's on our doorstep. We could come down here all the time and just spend the day lazing about." She suddenly grinned and dropped down to sit on her own towel, facing Caz. "And when we have the baby, we can bring them down here too and make memories."

Caz turned her head to look at her. "Yeah, that sounds nice." Her eyes were drawn to Grace's fingers slowly unbuttoning her blouse as she continued to talk.

"I used to love those days with Mum and Dad and Luke. We'd be so excited to get to the beach..." Her shirt opened as she squinted down at Caz again.

Her sunglasses were perched on top of her head, holding her hair up off of her face as she continued talking, "Not anything as nice as this one. We'd usually end up somewhere pebbly, and closer to home, like Shoreham, or Ferring, but still, we were kids. Didn't care about any of that."

Her shoulders appeared first, and then the material was fluttering downwards, and all Caz could focus on was the bellybutton ring. Because looking anywhere else would be problematic.

"And then we'd run straight into the water and..." Grace sighed. "It was just fun. I want that for our kids." When Caz didn't answer, she said, "Caz?"

"Uh, yes." Caz averted her gaze towards the sea. "Absolutely, and you know, I think a quick dip might be nice right now, too."

Grace nodded. "It is hot—might be good to get some salt water on us. I always get the best tan when I've been in the sea."

Caz stood up. "You know they put salt on pork to make crackling." She laughed, before ducking and running when Grace worked out what she'd just said and went to thump her.

"You had better not be comparing my delicate skin to

a pig, Caz Madden." She chased after her, laughing when Caz skipped into the water and jumped around as the heat of her skin was instantly frozen.

"It's freezing," Caz complained just as a wave hit, and she stumbled, falling into it.

"That's called karma." Grace laughed harder until Caz rose back up, and with both hands paddling water in her direction, Grace was soaked. "Oh, that's so mean…"

"You said you wanted to get wet," Caz chuckled, and continued to splash her.

"I didn't want to get that wet, and not like that." Grace faked a glare.

"Oh, and just how did you plan to get wet?"

The minute she'd said it, she froze. The implication of that statement had so many different variables, depending on how Grace had heard it.

And Grace's silence in the moment was worrying. No quick-witted, retaliatory response meant Caz panicked a little more.

"I thought I'd slowly dip in and out," Grace smiled, "but now, I've been overwhelmed and you're going to have to pay."

Unsure if there was any double meaning in that, Caz chose to ignore it. Overthinking right now would not do either of them any good. Snap out of it, she told herself, before turning and running deeper into the water.

"You'll have to catch me first," she shouted over her shoulder as Grace strode purposefully towards her.

"I already caught you. That's why I'm wearing this ring." Grace held up her hand, showing off her ring finger and then slowly folded it down and raised her middle one.

Caz laughed, normal service would resume.

CHAPTER SIXTEEN

Despite the heat of the day, a little too much sun burning the skin meant it felt a little chilly as the sun set. The sky was a glorious landscape of orange, purple, and red reflecting off of the sea.

Dinner had been a nice, quiet meal in town, at a restaurant where other couples and families filled the tables outside. Sipping a digestif, Caz couldn't help but notice the way Grace's face lit up anytime one of the toddlers smiled at her or screeched excitably.

"What?" Grace said, catching Caz smiling at her.

"Nothing, you just look happy."

Grace sat up, as though she'd just been praised for a top-notch essay. "Being with you makes me happy. Sometimes I wish —" She shook her head and looked away, out towards the water in the near distance.

"Wish what?" Caz asked, intrigued.

When Grace looked back at her, there were tears in her eyes.

"I just...sometimes I wish I was gay, so I could make you happy."

The words hit Caz in the chest as hard as a boulder that had rolled down a mountain, breaking apart and splintering into tiny, painful shards when it landed.

"I...I am happy." It wasn't a lie.

Grace nodded. "Yes, but..."

"No buts," Caz said. She reached out her hand and took Grace's. "I'm happy. Being with you, planning a future, gay or not, this is what I want."

"Is it? It's been a year, and you must be...needing that connection?"

Caz felt her cheeks burn. Was she that obvious? Had she said, or worse, done something that would infer she wanted something more?

"I don't," she said quickly...too quickly.

Grace chuckled. "You know, one of the things I love about you is that you're a rubbish liar."

Caz closed her eyes, swallowed slowly, and felt the heat burn hotter. "It's not that I want—"

"I would be okay with it, if you did," Grace offered.

Did she just suggest they sleep together? Rubbing at her face, Caz asked, "Okay with what, exactly?"

Lowering her voice, Grace said, "If you needed to, you know?"

"No, I don't know..."

"Tut." Grace sighed. "Look, all I am saying, is that if you need to get your needs met, then I'm okay with you going out and finding someone."

Caz wasn't sure what hurt more. That Grace was allowing her to go out and sleep with someone, or that it wasn't Grace offering to sleep with her. She turned the tables.

"And what about you? Are you suggesting this because it's something you want to do too?"

Grace looked horrified.

"No, not at all. God, no. I am quite capable of solving that issue all by myself, thank you." She chuckled but looked away quickly.

"Well, so am I," Caz responded. "Quite often, actually."

"Me too."

"Good, thanks for sharing." Caz smiled, taking the seriousness out of the conversation. She looked around for a waiter and then did the universal signal for the bill.

"You shared first." Grace grinned. She leaned forward. "How often is often?"

"Hold on, let me check my diary for you," Caz said with a hint of humourous sarcasm. She thumbed through the imaginary book and said, "Three times a week, and twice on Sunday."

"I'm glad your needs are being met," Grace added, just as the waiter placed the bill on the table.

She nabbed a mint chocolate from the small dish carrying the receipt and quicky unwrapped it while Caz checked the bill to make sure they weren't paying for anyone else's dinner.

Satisfied, Caz reached into her pocket and pulled her card free, placing it down on top.

"My needs are met," she said, gazing at Grace.

A small nod indicated Grace had heard her, but she said nothing further about it. Instead, she asked, "Are you eating that chocolate?"

CHAPTER SEVENTEEN

The following morning it was hot. Hotter than hot. The kind of heat you assumed greeted anyone heading down to hell for their initiation with the Devil kind of hot.

They'd found a spot on the beach a little further along from the previous day. It was quieter, the hint in the guest book at the house they'd rented had said. Just a few private houses and 'no parking' signs put people off, and most didn't walk this far once they hit the beach back at the touristy spot.

Towels were laid, the windbreaker and tent were in place, and Grace sat quietly, watching as Caz skipped the smaller waves like a kid.

When she was in past her knees, Caz turned and waved back at Grace in the same way Tom Hanks did in *Forrest Gump*. That made Grace giggle as she raised her hand and waved back.

The previous day's events still ran through her mind. The way Caz had tried so very hard not to stare at her as she'd undressed or the way Caz always seemed to take an extra second to think before speaking lately, as though she were making sure she said the correct thing and not what she was potentially about to blurt out.

Then she thought about their conversation last night. It would be so easy if she were gay. She loved Caz, there was no doubt of that. And her best friend was gorgeous. It wouldn't be hard to be attracted to her, especially as she was the best person on the planet for making Grace feel heard, seen, and loved. Would it be that different with a woman?

She scolded herself for having such ridiculous thoughts.

They'd been friends for almost twenty years. If there was going to be any moment when Caz might have looked at her in any way other than as a friend, it would have been back then, when they'd first met.

Maybe Caz had, and Grace just hadn't picked up on it? She could be oblivious to those kinds of things at times, but...she wasn't gay, so it wouldn't have mattered.

Would it?

She smiled as Caz finally dipped under the waves and then jumped up squealing before finally plunging back under and swimming around.

They were way too far into the friend zone now, *weren't they?*

This was why Grace had assumed that maybe Caz was just feeling a little lonely in the intimacy department, and why Grace had felt it was only fair to make her the offer.

But she hadn't expected the level of relief she had felt when Caz had declined to go off and sleep with someone else. And that unsettled her. *Why was she relieved?* This was her friend, and they'd agreed right at the start it was on the table as an option. Their marriage and commitment to each other was about family, love, and the future, not sex. Caz was free to engage in hook-ups.

And yet, Grace now realised, the idea of Caz going off with a stranger for a casual romp to satisfy her needs didn't sit well with her... Not well at all.

She thought of Macy, Caz's last girlfriend of any relative length of time. She'd lasted six months. Grace didn't like her much. Who was she kidding? She *really* didn't like her. She was far too immature for someone as grown up as Caz. And she always kept Caz waiting—late for every date. Grace had been glad when she'd got given the elbow.

Not that she ever encouraged Caz to dump these women; none of them were good enough for Caz as far as Grace was concerned. But she also couldn't, in retrospect, deny she wasn't just a little bit pleased when Caz was available to spend more time with her.

Was that selfish, or...something else?

"Jesus, what kind of friend are you?" she said to herself as she turned her face up towards the sunshine, letting the heat of it burn away the shame she felt for such thoughts.

"Hey, you coming in?" Caz said moments later, the shadow of her suddenly blocking out the sunlight. Tiny droplets of cold water landed on Grace's foot from Caz's dripping fingertips and raced each other down her hot skin.

God, she was adorable, wasn't she? Grace heard her own words in her head and smiled at the goosebumps appearing on Caz's body as she shivered a little in the breeze, or was it something else causing the reaction?

"Just so you can splash me and dunk me again?"

"Yep." Caz nodded, grinning at her. "You know you want it."

Grace swallowed hard. "I do?"

"Definitely. It's too hot. A quick, sudden burst of freezing English Channel will soon get you—"

"I think not," Grace said quickly, though right now a cold something might actually be what she needed to knock these thoughts out of her head.

Caz huffed and blew out a loud breath that ended with a "Pfft" as she flopped down onto her towel. "Are you alright?"

Grace frowned as she turned to face her. "Yes, why? What makes you ask that?"

Shrugging, Caz reached forward and let her fingers drag

through the sand. "Nothing, just...you've been quiet, so I'm just checking in."

Smiling now, Grace leaned over and kissed her cheek. "This is why I love you." *Because you put my every need first and focus all of that love in my direction, and I want it to be that way forever*, she caught herself thinking.

"That's okay then." Caz grinned. "Wanna build a sandcastle?"

"Yes, very much so," Grace said, as the words, *This is why I love you*, kept swimming around in her head. She watched Caz dig out an empty water bottle.

"Gonna fill this up and make the sand wet, then we can build a huge castle."

"You're such a kid." Grace laughed.

Caz was up and running to the water just as two women jogged along. They were side by side, in perfect step with one another, baseball caps on, sunglasses, too, but as they passed, Grace gasped.

They were long gone by the time Caz ran back and poured the water onto the dry sand.

"Did you see who that was?" Grace said excitedly and pointed. Caz followed her finger to see the back of two women running, getting further away with every step.

"Was it Kate Winslet? Did I bloody miss Kate Winslet?"

Grace shook her head. "No. It was that musician—the one who plays the piano and used to be in that band..."

"Which band?"

"The one from years ago. The bus crashed and—"

"Oh, that band...piano?" Caz wracked her brain. "Sasha?"

"Yes." Grace stabbed a finger at Caz. "Her, it was her, and I assume…isn't she gay?"

"One of the family, yes, I think I read that. I don't know her, though. Not my kind of music," Caz confirmed without the slightest interest in anyone famous who wasn't Kate Winslet.

"You need more water." Grace smiled, looking at the patch that was now drying already. "Lots of water."

CHAPTER EIGHTEEN

December 2024

It wasn't the merriest of Christmas mornings, and the breakfast had gone untouched, as Caz knew it would, but still, they were doing their best.

The tears in the shower had been the last of them, as though Grace had somehow been cleansed of all the sorrow that had consumed her in waves.

She'd gotten dressed and come downstairs to find Caz in the kitchen prepping lunch. Carrots were peeled and cut into halves and the potatoes were peeled and cut into quarters.

The small turkey joint was cooking in the oven.

George Michael sang *Last Christmas* on the speaker as Caz chopped up a white cabbage.

For a moment, Grace just stood there watching, torn between continuing that or doing what she wanted most to do. In the end, standing there felt more awkward, so she moved slowly until she was behind Caz and could reach around with her arms and hug her like a limpet.

"Hey," Caz greeted, dropping the knife to place her own hands over Grace's. "Glad you could make it."

"Do you need any help?"

"Not really, got it all under control," Caz said, picking up the knife again.

"Good, so I can stay here?" Grace asked, but they both already knew the answer.

"Yep. Just be prepared for dancing if the Pogues come on."

Grace chuckled, and for the second time that day, she felt something lift.

When Caz finished cutting the cabbage, she turned around and put her arms around Grace. Pulling her close until all Grace could do was breathe her in. The soft scents of washing detergent and a subtle cologne that had become Caz's trademark scent over the years were all she needed to know she was loved and safe.

"Wanna watch *Elf*?" Caz asked, kissing the top of her head.

"Only if you're watching it with me." Grace looked up into the eyes of someone she knew would walk through fire for her.

"Yeah, like I'm going to miss that." Caz pulled a silly face. "I was thinking... I know everyone always has Christmas dinner in the afternoon, but why don't we switch it up and have picky bits now, and then dinner later?"

"Make our own traditions?"

"Yep. So, you go sort the TV and get the film lined up, while I get together a smorgasbord of snacks and, ooh, mince pies?"

Grace's eyes went wide. "Oh, now you're just too much," she laughed, "but yes, with brandy cream."

"On its way," Caz said, freeing her from the hug and twirling away towards the fridge and all of the goodies she'd bought in hope that, somehow, they would enjoy Christmas.

Rockin' Around the Christmas Tree came on and Grace watched as Caz began to move her hips in time and sing along with the lyrics.

It wasn't going to be the Christmas they'd planned, but right now she was hopeful, and having Caz by her side made that all the more easier to focus on a brighter new year.

CHAPTER NINETEEN

That night, Caz finished washing up the mugs that were still warm from the last mouthfuls of the hot chocolate they'd held just moments earlier.

She glanced around the kitchen. Everything was tidy, clean, and ready for a new day. Leaving the room, she switched the light off and then did the same quick glance around the lounge.

Everything was in its place, just how it should be.

At the bottom of the stairs, she looked up before letting herself finally release the pent-up tension in one long breath. This had not been the day she had planned, and yet, in a lot of ways, despite the sadness that lingered for them both, it had been nice.

Her left foot raised and she took the first step, climbing each one until she was at the top, standing in the silence on the landing. She listened for any sign that Grace was in any discomfort, but when no evidence came, she turned and walked into her own room.

Without turning the light on, she pulled her clothes off. Feeling for the towel that hung on the back of the door, she pulled it around her body and quickly stepped back into the hallway and then into the bathroom.

One long shower later, teeth brushed, and her hair pulled into a loose bun, she pulled on her pyjamas. Raising the duvet, she slid into bed and got settled.

Dreams drifted in, but the inevitable need to pee woke her

up a few hours later. Tossing the duvet back, she was grateful for the thermal pyjamas, but she still shivered as her feet hit the carpet.

Ablutions sorted, Caz was about to enter her bedroom again when she heard it—the soft whimpering. She crept back along the landing and stood outside of Grace's door, listening.

Her hand rested on the door handle and she let her forehead land softly on the door. The urge to rush in and comfort being held back by the fear of being told to get lost.

Logically, she knew that wouldn't happen out of any malice, but maybe Grace didn't want her running to her rescue every time she was upset. That was the conclusion she was coming to when the weeping quieted, and she hoped that maybe, Grace had fallen asleep. But in the next breath, an almighty sob rang out and Caz could hold back no longer.

She pushed down on the handle and the door sprung open. Without a word, she padded barefoot across the room, not waiting for an invitation. She lifted the covers and climbed into the bed, pulling Grace towards her and wrapping herself as closely around her friend as she could.

"It's okay," Caz said between shushing noises. Her body rocked them both and Grace's fingers gripped the front of Caz's pyjama top while the sobs continued.

"I really...I really thought..." Grace stuttered out, her breathing ragged as the tears fell and her chest heaved in air. "I... the...I really thought..."

Whatever it was she thought, Caz never got to the bottom of.

"Don't leave...me," Grace said, tightening her grip.

"I won't. I'm not going anywhere," Caz promised.

CHAPTER TWENTY

June 2025

Caz lounged on the sofa in nothing more than boxer shorts and a vest. Even at eight o'clock, it was still hotter outside than Mount Vesuvius. A fan blew and moved slowly as it oscillated one way and then the other. The bowl of ice sitting beneath it had helped to create a bit of air conditioning, but it was still fidgety hot.

From the kitchen, she could hear Grace singing to herself as she went about creating a salad. Caz hoped there was some chicken, too, from the smell that was drifting in. Her stomach rumbled to confirm the desire.

"Do you need a hand?" she called out. Her head twisted to the side so she could hear Grace, but she needn't have worried as her friend swanned into the room carrying two bowls.

"No, all done, but I left you the washing up." Grace smiled and handed down a bowl. "Shift up," she said, already preparing to perch herself onto the couch beside Caz.

"This smells awesome."

"It does. I tried that new meat rub you bought—the lemon and fennel."

"Beats going out any day." Caz harpooned a cherry tomato with her fork and shoved it quickly into her mouth. "I think... you're the best salad maker I know."

Grace scoffed. "It's just salad."

"Nope, it's not *just* anything. You put things in it I'd never think about." She moved her fork about and hit a chickpea, raising it as evidence. "Like this, and the dressing. You always make amazing dressings."

Grace sat back a little further and leaned against one of Caz's bent knees.

"You're just so easy to please."

Caz nodded. "I guess, but equally, you are amazing."

"Are you like this with all of your other girlfriends?" Grace asked before realising how that sounded. "I mean—"

"You're my wife. None of them made it to that status." Caz winked and stabbed at a chunk of avocado smothered in grated carrot. "But yeah, if you mean am I supportive, caring, and the kind of woman who wants to make sure her partner feels loved, then yeah..."

"You do certainly manage that," Grace said, before another question hit her. "Do I do that...for you, I mean? Do I make sure you feel loved?"

Caz placed the fork into the bowl and the bowl into her lap. "Yes. Every day." She smiled. "You do stuff for me that I wouldn't think to do."

"Like what?"

"I've never had to clean the bathroom. You've wiped it all down before I even think about it. My lunch is made and ready for me to just grab out of the fridge, and I love the little notes that have smiley faces or a silly joke. They make me smile when I open up the box and see them."

Grace smiled at that.

"And you call me out on stuff, make me think about things from a different perspective, and give me time to work things out without us needing a row."

"Do you think it's weird that we don't really argue,

though?"

Caz picked up her fork again. "No."

"I've never had a relationship where we didn't row," Grace mused, "like, full-on screaming at one another."

Grimacing, Caz put her fork back down. "I mean, yeah, I guess, but it's different with you."

"I know what you mean, but why is that, do you think?"

"We did have that one big row, though," Caz reminded her. "You didn't speak to me for two days."

"It was two hours." Grace laughed. "Don't exaggerate." She smiled. "I'd forgotten about that."

"I haven't."

CHAPTER TWENTY-ONE

October 2024

Halloween was in full effect. Caz had decorated the front garden with skeletons climbing from graves and ghosts swooping down off the roof, much to Grace's disapproval. She wasn't a fan of such things, but it had always made Caz happy, so she'd shut up and let her enjoy it.

But getting home to find a full-on Halloween party she hadn't even been invited to, taking place in the living room, was a bit much.

"*It was a graveyard smash,*" several voices sang out.

Grace breathed deeply, thrust her key into the lock, and was just about to go inside when a group of kids ran up the path screaming, "Trick or treat," at her.

It made her jump, and she spun around just in time to get an egg thrown at her. "Too slow."

They laughed and ran off.

"Fuckers," Grace seethed, as yolk dripped down the side of her head. She got the door open just as Caz was dancing her way out of the kitchen with three bottles of lager in her hands, laughing as she joined in with the singing.

"*It was the monster ma—*" Coming to a halt, Caz laughed nervously. "Oh, hey, babe, we're just..." She spotted the egg and instantly sobered. "Are you alright?"

"Really?" Grace's sarcasm dripped like the egg, her lips pursed, eyes staring hard at Caz.

She didn't get to say anything further before Dani made her way out of the living room. "Hey, where's those drin—oops," she said, turning instantly and heading back into the safety of the lounge.

Grace looked through and saw Portia wearing a Frankenstein forehead hat, talking to two women Grace didn't recognise.

Hot women.

The doorbell rang, and the standoff continued until Caz put the drinks down on the stairs and picked up a huge skull-shaped bucket filled with sweets.

"Um, I let the kids know they could knock," she said, gingerly making her way around Grace to open the door. "I'd better answer it before the entire house gets egged."

Grace picked up two of the bottles just as Caz glanced back quickly at her, before the doorbell rang again and she opened it.

"Hey, Gertie, wow, that's such a fab outfit."

Grace stomped up the stairs, mumbling to herself, "Supposed to be our home, not a bloody frat house."

She'd already downed half of the first bottle by the time she'd slammed her bedroom door shut. It didn't make any sense. Caz had never been the party girl, and yet lately, every other night was some kind of reason for her friends to be over, drinking beer and making too much noise.

She wasn't a party pooper, but all Grace wanted to do after a long day was get home, have a bath, and relax in front of the TV with some dinner. *Was that too much to ask for?*

Pulling her hair tie out, she shook her hair free. Then she divested herself of the office uniform suit and blouse and pulled her dressing gown around her.

It was just gone six according to her watch, which itself

was placed down on the countertop next to the bottles of lager.

She finished the rest of the bottle she'd started, picked up the second one, and left her room. A bath would still be good. Crossing the landing, she noted the music had stopped at least.

She closed the door and locked it.

Putting the second bottle down on the corner of the bath, Grace twisted the taps until she had the temperature she wanted, flowing as furiously as her temper. A healthy pour of her favourite bubble bath, and she finally unclenched her jaw.

Voices in the hall were muffled, and then the sound of the door closing gave the impression Caz had called an early night.

Just as Grace sank down into the water, there was a knock on the door.

"Grace?" Caz said gently. "I...uh...did you want dinner?"

Rolling her eyes, Grace sank lower, madder than she'd ever been in the entire time she'd known Caz.

But she couldn't fathom why.

Was it the noise and the beer and the friends...or was it the two hot women she had never met before?

CHAPTER TWENTY-TWO

When she came downstairs, Caz looked around. Beer cans littered the coffee table. Now, she saw it through Grace's eyes and sighed at herself.

The party hadn't been planned. The electricity had gone out at work. Ron had given them all the afternoon off and she'd allowed herself to be dragged by Dani to the bar.

Dragged willingly, she had to admit, and maybe that had been her downfall. There had been a few nights with the girls over for pizza, but it had been a while since she'd really let her hair down.

They'd called Portia, who turned up with Dalilah and two women they were kind of hoping to date. Dani and Caz had never met either of them before. They were nice enough, though, and the afternoon had been fun.

She shook her head at herself and began picking up the debris. Then she kicked herself again. There was nothing for dinner. Had the tables been turned and Grace had come home early, she'd have thought about Caz and put together a meal for her.

Instead, Caz had treated the day like a party. And worse, she'd made Grace feel uncomfortable.

A timely reminder that this wasn't just her home, was it?

"Dick move, Madden."

Beer cans cleared, she ordered pizza and made sure the lounge looked immaculate just in time for Grace coming back down the stairs; hair up, fluffy slippers on her feet, and the big dressing gown over plaid pyjamas.

"Alright?" Caz asked tentatively as she watched her.

Grace ignored the question and walked straight past and into the kitchen with Caz following.

"Look, I know, I should have asked first. It was totally out of order to just bring everyone home, but the silent treatment isn't—"

Grace glared at her. "I'm not giving you the silent treatment."

Caz raised a brow but didn't push the point.

"The electrics went out at work and your dad sent us all home and—"

Huffing, Grace said, "You invited half the world into our home for a gangbang?"

Caz stared. "A gangbang?" She almost laughed, the idea was so ridiculous, but the look on Grace's face told her that would be a very bad thing to do if she wanted to stay married. "We just went to the pub and then I thought that was a bit—I didn't think you'd be impressed with me coming home late, so I made the stupid mistake of inviting them back here, and—"

"I might have said that I had no issue with you getting your needs met elsewhere when the occasion arose, but I didn't expect you'd be bringing them home to rub it in my face," Grace exploded. "Honestly, could you be any less subtle?"

"Woah." Caz held her hands up. "I didn't...I mean...nope." She laughed nervously. "You thought Lori and Kay were... Oh my God," she said to herself as she realised what it all looked like. "No, not at all. I would never do that to you. They were Portia and Dalilah's dates. Me and Dani—we were just having a drink."

"Sounded like a party, Caz." Grace had softened, but she wasn't ready to let the anger diffuse completely.

"I know. We got some beers from the shop and then... You know what it's like when you've got a nice buzz going. I just put the music on and...honestly, I thought you'd join us." Her head dropped. "I didn't think whether you'd had a bad day."

"I didn't have a bad day, but it was exhausting. I just wanted to come home, have a bath, and then cosy up on the sofa with you. Instead, I find half the pub in here," she sighed, "and some little shits threw an egg at me."

"Which little shits?" Caz felt her hackles rise. "I'll go and find them and—" She was already moving towards the door.

The move threw Grace out of her anger. Suddenly, she felt an overwhelming sense of emotions, the whole thing escalating into an eruption of tears.

"Wait, Caz, don't."

"I'm not having them hurting you. I don't care if it's an egg or—" She spun around. "Grace?" Retracing her steps, Caz rushed back to the kitchen and pulled Grace closer. "What's wrong?"

"I don't know, I think it's my hormones, I'm due on and I just wanted a bath and to relax and—"

The doorbell rang.

"Hold that thought, it's the pizza." Caz smiled. "Can we start this night over?"

Grace nodded. "I don't want to fight with you."

"Me either," Caz said over her shoulder. She reached the door and flung it open.

A man standing there, holding out a pizza box said, "Pizza," as though it wasn't obvious.

"Yeah, thanks." She took it from him and closed the door.

Turning back, she found Grace holding out a bottle of lager. Their first fight was over.

CHAPTER TWENTY-THREE

June 2025

The couch was smaller than their own at home. Not as wide or long. The length wasn't that much of an issue. Legs could bend, and feet could hang over, but with a lot less width, it meant, when Grace got comfortable, Caz had to play big spoon, because her arm had been needed around Grace's waist to make sure she didn't roll off.

"I could just sit in the armchair." Grace giggled when the arm tightened its grip.

"You can't, not after I've contorted myself into this position to fit you in," Caz said half-seriously. She was squeezed up against the back of the sofa, knees bent, and her feet tucked under the cushions. Her other arm was squished underneath Grace's cushion, her head resting on top.

"Good, because I'm quite comfortable and it feels a little chilly now the sun's gone down."

"More like because you've caught the sun today. Your shoulders are still pink."

"It was such a nice day," Grace said dreamily. "I can't wait until we have a kid or two running around. We can take them to the beach and you can build sandcastles with them."

The film played on. Neither of them really paying it much attention. Caz felt her eyes grow heavy and was drifting in and out.

So relaxed.

"What do you think?" she heard Grace ask.

"Huh, what? Sorry, I drifted off then."

Grace chuckled and wriggled closer. "I was thinking, this is nice, laying like this together, and maybe...it could work for when we get the sperm and you—"

Caz stiffened, fully awake now.

This wasn't a conversation she was expecting this evening, or any evening before they got home, and the subject would inevitably be raised again.

"How do you mean?"

"I just thought it might be less...invasive for you. I could —" Without warning, Grace raised her left leg and hooked it backwards until her foot rested on Caz's calf. "And you could then—" she reached for Caz's hand and moved it backwards too, "slide under my leg and do it, while holding me, but without the —"

Caz understood what she was saying. It actually made a lot of sense and definitely would remove a level of embarrassment, while creating a whole heap more.

"Yeah, okay, I get it...would that work...you know, for you?"

"I think so." She brought her leg down and reached for Caz's hand again, slipping it back around herself until Caz was holding her close. "I don't mind, really, I trust you, but I appreciate that it's not something one does for a friend usually. I want you to be part of the process, from start to finish, though."

"I guess I just always thought... I didn't really think I'd ever have kids, and I never considered what the process would be if I did. I just assumed it would be clinical, with doctors. And I think about friends who have had kids and how...I dunno, but it must have been more..."

"Loving?" Grace ventured.

"Yeah, I suppose. Two people who loved one another so much they wanted to make a baby, and then they did so because they were able to be romantic like that with each other and—"

"Do you want us to be romantic when we do it?" Grace asked, and just the words sent a tumble of butterflies roiling in her tummy.

"In an ideal world—"

"We could," Grace interjected. "I mean...there's nothing stopping us from doing that."

The words wouldn't catch up in Caz's head. What did she mean by they could?

"I'm not following," Caz admitted.

In a moment of acrobatic amazement, Grace twisted until she was facing Caz, noses almost touching.

"You've kissed me before," she said, and Caz swallowed hard.

"I was drunk, and don't even remember doing it."

Grace smiled. "True, but I have admitted it was a good kiss. I didn't dislike it."

Was this really happening? Caz thought. Was this something new between them or just a proposal for making Caz feel more at ease impregnating her best friend?

"What are you saying?"

Grace rolled her eyes and grinned. "I'm saying, if I were facing you and—" She raised her leg again, opening herself to the position that might work for them. "We could kiss while you—you know."

Her eyes lingered on Caz for so long that Caz felt mesmerised.

"I don't think that would—"

"Kiss me," Grace insisted, moving closer.

"What? No, I can't…"

"Can't, or don't want to?" Grace asked. "I get it, if you don't want to, I'm sorry if I emb—"

Her words were cut short by a finger touching her lips.

"Can you just give me a moment to think?"

They were too close. And with an invitation to get closer with Grace staring at her like that, she couldn't stop herself. It just happened. Their lips touched and then her tongue was met with Grace's, and they were kissing.

"I need—" Caz pulled back before she did something with her hands that would really ruin things.

Somehow, she managed to wriggle free and climb out from where she'd been pinned.

"I'll be back in a minute."

Grace rolled over and grinned up at her. "Alright."

CHAPTER TWENTY-FOUR

It only took a few minutes for Caz to walk to the beach. At gone nine, it still wasn't fully dark, though the sun had almost disappeared from sight. There was just a faint glow of oranges and yellows in the sky. The moon hadn't made an appearance yet, but it would soon enough.

Caz marched through the sandier part of the beach until she hit the more solid and stable sand that had been soaked by the sea and dried out. She kept marching until her bare feet were washed over by the cold water as it rushed in and out.

She felt a shiver as her body temperature dropped with every step as she strolled the shore, her mind awash with thoughts and feelings that were becoming more difficult to keep under control.

Every image of Grace flashed through her mind: The wedding. Christmas. Her smile. Her tears.

All of it had built a huge reaction within Caz to protect and love her more than ever.

"Hello...excuse me?" a voice called out and brought her from her thoughts. Caz turned quickly and found a woman looking at her.

Dark curly hair tied back, her arms wrapped around herself. Another woman, older, stood a little further back, looking on and watching them both.

"Are you okay?" she asked, and Caz frowned.

"Yeah, I'm good. Thanks," Caz called back with a half-wave.

"We just don't see many people walking..." The woman stepped closer and eyed Caz up and down. "By themselves at night. Are you sure you're alright?"

The woman seemed genuine and something about her concern had unlocked Caz in a way nobody but Grace ever had.

"My wife just kissed me," she blurted out without thinking about how crazy that sounded.

The woman's eyes widened. "Okay." She then smiled. "And that's a bad thing?"

Caz looked back along the beach and sighed. "I'm not sure. I mean, I wanted her to, but...it opens doors to things, doesn't it?"

"It does, yes," the woman said slowly as she gazed down at Caz's hand and the ring on her finger.

She was right in front of Caz now. She looked like a grown-up, one of those women who had their shit together, *Like Grace*, Caz thought.

"Sorry." Caz laughed. "That must sound completely ridiculous."

"A little, but not the craziest thing I've ever heard." She held her hand out. "Morgan."

"Sweetheart, everything alright?" the woman behind her called out, and Caz stepped back as Morgan turned and waved.

"Yes, all fine, darling." Morgan turned back to Caz, "We're getting married later this year."

"Cool. You'll love it," Caz answered.

Morgan frowned. "I'm allowed to kiss her already, though."

Caz blew out a breath, nervous laughter erupting.

"You can talk to me, if...if you want to." She turned back to the house. "Come on, we've got wine, or coffee, water...a fire pit." She began to walk away.

It took only a moment of thought before Caz found herself following. Afterall, who else did she have to talk about this with? Dani would have a field day, if after everything Caz had said and done, it ended up with her admitting it was all a sham, but now it was becoming difficult.

The house was beautiful.

All glass and wooden decks with big comfortable chairs around a glowing fire. For the first time, Caz began to wonder who exactly she was talking to.

"This is Alex," Morgan said, as the older woman reappeared. She had a scarf wrapped around her head, all bohemian in a flowing gown. She handed Caz a blanket and smiled.

"Hello..."

"Sorry, yes, Caz...Caroline, but Caz to everyone I know... unless I'm in trouble." She chuckled and looked again at Alex. There was something familiar about her.

"Caz has an unusual predicament," Morgan explained to Alex.

"Oh, and what would that be?" Alex sat down opposite and smiled up at Morgan when the younger woman rested her palm on her shoulder.

"Her wife...kissed her."

There was an amused look on Alex's face as she understood the dilemma.

"See, when you say it like that I realise how ridiculous it sounds." Caz laughed and accepted a glass and the offer of some wine, which wasn't her favourite, but she wasn't going to be rude.

"So, what's the story?" Alex urged.

Caz sighed. "I married my best friend." Their faces did that thing that said, "*Aww.*" "My straight, best friend." And the faces changed to that thing that says, "*Oh.*" "Yeah, and so, it was meant to be an arrangement. We both wanted kids, but relationships were just not working out, and so…when Grace suggested it, I figured why not. We love each other."

"But she's straight and you're…"

"I'm gay, yeah, it's a non-sexual relationship, it was never supposed to be—"

"But now she wants you to kiss her?" Morgan asked, settling down on the arm of Alex's chair.

Caz nodded. "I mean, we've always been close, you know. Like most friends, we'd always snuggle up on the sofa to watch TV. In every other way, we're the perfect couple," she laughed gently, "but lately…I dunno, I'm starting to feel things I didn't think I felt."

"And she's encouraging it," Alex stated rather than asked.

"Why did she offer?" Morgan quizzed. "Was there something that brought it up?"

"Yeah. We're trying for a baby, and last time it didn't work. This time, she wants to try and do it more…naturally—bypass the clinical aspects of it and find a donor and then…" Caz blew her breath out again. "She wants me to do it."

Both sets of watching eyebrows raised.

"And because I was reticent about…that part of it, she started talking about positions we could use that would make it easier and then she asked if it would be easier if it was more romantic."

"In an ideal world, do you think maybe you'd like it to be romantic with Grace?" Alex leaned forward as she asked the question.

"I love her. I love her with every fibre, but the idea of losing her because we ruined everything over something that's not real...I couldn't risk that."

"Maybe the risk would be worth it?" Morgan said.

"What if it *was* real?" Alex added.

CHAPTER TWENTY-FIVE

Returning to the cottage, Caz opened the door and found Grace sitting on the sofa looking up at her, a slightly worried look on her face that eased the moment she laid eyes on Caz.

"Alright?" she asked. "You've been gone ages. I was starting to worry. You didn't take your phone."

Caz nodded. "Sorry, I got caught up…"

"Caught up?"

"I went for a walk on the beach and then this nice couple… I think they were worried about me, so they invited me to sit with them and talk…"

Grace stood up and eyed her up and down. "You went off with complete strangers and told them what, exactly?" There was now a lightly bemused look on her face.

"Was that not okay?" Caz asked hesitantly. She hadn't considered if it was bad. In fact, it had done her a world of good being able to offload her thoughts and hear them answered by someone else's logic.

Grace's lips began to turn upward, revealing those little dimples that Caz loved. "You do know you went out in your vest and pants, right?"

Caz froze for a moment, before slowly glancing down at herself, and the bare arms and legs that hadn't felt anything but the late summer heat and the fire pit. She was wearing a pair of black, snugly fitting boy shorts with the words 'Hot Stuff' written on them and a white vest, that at least hadn't had any holes or oil stains.

"Oh, the shame." She clapped a hand over her mouth and stifled a laugh. "That'll be why they seemed a bit...I think they might have thought I was about to throw myself into the sea."

"I didn't think kissing me was that bad." Grace smiled.

"No it wasn't that, it was—"

She stared at Grace and the giggle she'd stifled began to escape. Grace mirrored her and before they knew it, they were both doubled over and falling into each other on the couch.

When Caz stopped laughing enough, she swung a leg and captured Grace between her thighs, allowing her friend to lean back against her, enjoying the sensation of Grace's shoulders still moving as her giggles began to subside.

"So, I thought about what you said." Caz offered a segue way into the conversation they needed to have.

"Kissing me?" Grace said it so naturally that it soothed Caz a little. It wasn't going to be a big deal either way.

"Yeah, and although it wasn't repulsive—"

Grace elbowed her in the ribs. "I should think not."

Laughing, Caz continued, "I just mean that...you said you don't want it to feel clinical this time, and yet, for me, that's how it would feel. I can't just kiss someone on demand. I can't plan it. Kissing someone is something organic."

Grace turned onto her hip. "I get that. I guess I didn't really see it from that perspective." She shrugged a little. "I think maybe I've been putting too much pressure on you, and that's not fair." She turned again and leaned back how she had been moments earlier. "Maybe I can just do it myself, the fiddly part. And we could just be like this, with you holding me."

"I can do that," Caz answered, with a kiss to the top of her head.

"And I'm glad you found someone to talk to. Maybe you

should confide the truth to someone closer. It might be what you need."

Caz slid her arms around Grace. "The only person I tell my secrets to, is you. You've always been my rock—my shoulder to lean on. That hasn't changed. If anything, it makes it more special. I know I can find it difficult to express myself in the moment sometimes, but you always give me the space I need to process it and…nobody else gets that."

"Well, I am your wife, after all," Grace joked.

"And I'm glad you are," Caz said in all seriousness. Because she was. She'd never been surer of anything in her life. There was no way she was going to ruin what they had together.

"I'm going to bed." Grace yawned.

"Yeah, I think I am too," Caz said before the inevitable catching yawn found its way to her. "Lead the way."

CHAPTER TWENTY-SIX

January 2025

It hadn't gone unnoticed that sleeping together in the same bed had become the norm for them both. A silent agreement that hadn't needed to be asked; they'd just fallen into the routine of it.

The first few nights, Caz had just followed Grace to bed and laid there with her while she cried. Sometimes, Caz had cried too, both mourning the loss of something that had never been more than an imagined dream. And each time, they'd woken up wrapped in one another.

Nothing more was said about it.

Until now.

Grace moved around the kitchen with an ease that hadn't been there much lately. She pulled ingredients from the fridge and chopped vegetables into small pieces on the chopping board with the huge cleaver that always made Caz feel a little bit apprehensive to use. Yet Grace chopped and chopped away as though it were the tiniest blade.

"I was thinking..." Grace remained facing her task and not Caz. "Should we just move your things into my room now?"

The question took Caz aback for a moment. It wasn't what she'd been expecting as she sat on the stool peeling potatoes.

But now it was asked, she knew there wasn't really anything to think about.

It made sense.

"I suppose I could. If that's what you—"

Grace put the cleaver down and turned to face Caz. Her eyes steely but damp, as though she were holding back the emotions that had freely overspilled recently.

"I do...I—I like you being there. I feel...safe," she admitted, before spinning back around and picking up the chopper again.

"Okay, then," Caz said. She heard herself speak the words, and wondered why it was that it was so easy to say them, but she wasn't given any more time to linger on her thoughts before Grace jumped back, crying out.

"Shit," she hissed, dropping the cleaver and holding a finger in her other hand. Blood oozed through the gaps.

"Uh, okay. Don't panic," Caz said, definitely trying not to panic. She wasn't good with gore and blood and medical things. "How bad is it?" she asked, one eye firmly closed, the other barely squinting in Grace's direction.

"I just nicked my finger." Grace grimaced and took a peek. "I won't die but....I might need a stitch of two."

"Oh, bloody hell, Gracie." Caz grabbed her keys and found a clean tea towel in the drawer. "Hold your hand out."

The minute Grace did, the blood ran faster. Caz felt her stomach lurch as she quickly wrapped the towel around the wound. "Hold," she instructed, before heading to the freezer and grabbing a handful of ice. Unwrapping the towel halfway, she placed the ice inside and then rewrapped it. "Cold should slow the blood flow."

"How do you know that?" Grace quizzed.

"Your dad sent us all on a first aid course. You know what mechanics are like for cutting themselves."

Grace nodded. It made perfect sense.

"Right, coat on and hospital." Caz guided Grace out into

the hallway and to the door. Pulling coats from the hooks and holding one up for Grace to slip her arms into. She bundled her out the door and pressed the fob to release the doors on the car.

"Hi." Felicity from next door waved at them. "Happy New Year."

Caz waved quickly back. "And to you." She jumped in before Felicity, or Flick, as she'd informed them she liked to be called, got into a conversation. The woman was nice, but she could blab on far too much for Caz's liking.

Grace waved from inside the car as Caz engaged the ignition and started the car.

"Saved by the lack of interest?" Grace laughed.

"Was I rude?" Caz asked. "I didn't mean to be...but you know what she's like..." She glanced at Grace. "Hand in the air, keep your hand—" She leaned across the car and pulled the seatbelt around Grace, before taking the injured hand and placing it against her own shoulder. "Gravity," she finished knowingly and Grace just smiled at her.

"At least I am in safe hands."

CHAPTER TWENTY-SEVEN

June 2025

Grace studied her phone with a seriousness Caz hadn't seen for a while.

Smiling.

Reading.

Frowning.

Flicking the screen to move the page on to the next.

And then she sighed. "It's so difficult."

Caz nodded and handed her a mug of steaming, freshly brewed tea. "Yup. And I thought we weren't going to think about it 'til after we got home?" she said, sitting down beside her and taking the phone from her hands.

Caz glanced quickly at the screen before she clicked off the website and put the phone down onto the sofa between them. "These are donors with the clinic."

"I was just looking." Grace grinned. "I'm excited about it."

"I know you are," Caz acknowledged, placing her hand on Grace's knee. "But...we need to enjoy our time here and staying cooped up looking at phones trying to decide whose sperm we want to buy, is not my idea of fun when the sun is shining and we have a beach within walking distance."

"You've changed your mind, haven't you?" Grace said with just the barest hint of frustration in her tone.

"No, that's not—"

Grace sat up abruptly. "If you have, it's best you say now."

"Grace," Caz said firmly, "I haven't changed my mind. I just want to enjoy this time together like we planned, without the stress we know will inevitably come when we do sit down and make a decision about who we use...together."

Grace sighed again, more heavily this time. "You're right. Sorry. I just—I didn't think it would hurt to have a quick look."

"We've got two more days to just chill and relax, which is the best place you can be before entering into this and making any attempt at getting pregnant."

"You're right, so, what do you want to do? Beach again?"

Caz jumped up, grabbed her car keys and wallet from the table beside her. "No, it's almost lunchtime. Let's go into town and get something to eat and have a wander around the shops." She smiled. "We can hit the beach this afternoon when we need to cool off with a swim."

"Lunch sounds good." Grace checked her watch, 11.15 a.m. By the time they drove into town it would be midday and she was definitely feeling hungry enough for some food. "There's a—"

"The Gantry?" Caz grinned. It was Grace's favourite fancy restaurant chain. "I know...I booked us a table."

"You did?"

"Yeah, it's your favourite." Caz shrugged.

Grace kissed Caz's blushing cheek. "You're the only one who remembers things like that."

Taking her hand, Caz twirled Grace around. "Then that... is a travesty."

Her spin coming to a stop, Grace fell against Caz, laughing until she looked up and into Caz's eyes. "I like it. You see me. You've always seen me."

"Hard to miss, to be fair."

Grace's eyes narrowed. "Are you comparing me to a pig again?" She smiled at her own joke, her palms settling warmly against Caz's chest.

"Nope…more like a peacock…in all its glory."

"Nice save." Grace grinned. Her palms patted gently before she took a breath and stepped away. "Shall we go?"

Caz did a roll of her hand, bowing as she said, "After you, M'Lady."

CHAPTER TWENTY-EIGHT

Caz parked the car as close to the high street as they could get, but far enough away from the restaurant that it gave Grace enough time and options to peruse some of the shops.

It didn't take long before Caz was loaded up like a pack horse with multiple bags of things her wife just had to have, including, she noticed, a baby's romper suit with an image of a car on the front.

She didn't comment on it. What was the point? Dampening Grace's excitement just seemed so counterproductive, and anyway, they'd probably need it soon enough.

"Are you done? Because the table is booked, and we still have to get there." Caz checked her watch once more.

Threading her arm around Caz's elbow, Grace tightened her grip and looked up at her, smiling. "Yep. For now."

"Good, because I might just die of starvation…and heat stroke… I'm not a camel," Caz said with a seriousness she couldn't keep up. The corners of her mouth turned upwards as she gazed down at Grace.

Arm in arm, they strolled along the cobbled part of the street. Grace had taken several bags from Caz's grip and they swung easily by her side with every step she took.

When they reached the restaurant, Caz stepped forward to open the door, but felt herself tugged back as Grace's hand slid down her arm and their fingers entwined.

"What's up?" she asked quickly, alarmed at the way Grace

looked at her.

Grace's features moved from a subtle frown, her lips pressed together tightly, before something else must have come to mind and her face relaxed into a smile.

"Nothing," she said quietly. "I'm just..." She shrugged easily. "Happy." The smile widened. "And I just wanted to tell you that without it sounding..." Now her nose scrunched, alongside another shrug. "Silly."

Caz let the door close and stepped towards Grace. It felt natural to just...kiss her.

Grace didn't complain. It wasn't like the kiss they'd shared previously, but it wasn't the kind of kiss you shared with a friend, either.

"If there is one thing I am sure of...it's that marrying you was the best decision I've ever made, and it will be my life's honour to make sure you always feel...silly." Caz grinned. "Now, food. I am hungry."

"Okay, okay." Grace laughed and squeezed under Caz's arm when she held the door open. "You're an idiot, you know that?"

"I'm your idiot. That's all that matters." She smiled, before her attention moved to the woman behind the desk. "Hi, table for Madden."

A quick perusal of the dining room plan, and the woman reached for menus. "Right this way."

Grace followed, Caz taking up the rear of the formation, her mind doing mental somersaults, as Grace's words played out.

But more than that, it was the way Grace had been looking at her lately; the way they were kissing now, and the way she was currently looking at Grace, too. Her eyes drifted lower to enjoy the way Grace's backside moved in those tight jeans.

Caz breathed deeply and looked away—to the floor and

then around the room. Two sets of friendly eyes stared over at her.

A hand raised and waved.

She recognised Morgan instantly. Alex looked different without her headscarf, but still, who else could it be?

"Hi," Caz said, thankful for something to take her mind off of that perfect backside. She was about to ask a stupid question —"*What are you doing here?*" Bloody obvious, wasn't it? Instead, she just kind of nodded and continued to follow the waitress and Grace.

When they were seated, Grace leaned in.

"Did you just say hi to them?"

Caz nodded. "Yeah, it's polite, isn't it?"

Grace's eyes grew wide. "You know who that is, don't you?"

Caz nodded. "Yeah, Alex and Morgan," she said, nonchalantly picking up the menu and giving it no further mind until she felt a kick under the table. "Ow, what was that for?"

Grace was still staring at her with wide, questioning eyes. "I'm sorry, what?"

Caz stared at her nonplussed. "They're the women I spoke to on the beach last night."

"Sometimes I think you are the most oblivious person on the planet," Grace hissed quietly. "That's Sasha, the pianist... we saw them on the beach—" She stopped for second and then continued, "I saw them on the beach and told you...she's hella famous."

"Well, she's hella nice, then," Caz responded, and continued to read the menu.

Grace reached over and pulled the menu down. "You really aren't the slightest bit excited about the fact that you know them?"

"I don't know them. I met them and had a drink and a chat with them." She closed the menu again. "They're just normal people. Do you want to meet her? I'll introduce you."

"What? No, that would be...silly."

Caz grinned. "Well, it is my life's work to let you be silly."

CHAPTER TWENTY-NINE

Caz got up before Grace could say another word and made her way over to where Alex and Morgan were sitting and watching with an amused look on their faces.

"Hello," Caz said, only feeling a little awkward, now she was actually standing in front of them. "So, Grace informs me that I'm culturally out of step and must be an idiot for not knowing who I was talking to the other night."

It was Morgan who spoke. "I don't recognise her half the time, and I live with her."

Caz smiled, grateful for the comradeship.

"Are you having a romantic lunch, or would you like to join us?" Alex asked, throwing a playing wink into the mix.

"Thank you, we wouldn't want to intrude, but..." She glanced back at Grace. "I think she's dying to say hello."

Alex laughed. "I'll be over in a moment." She picked up her glass and raised it as she looked behind Caz and towards Grace. "She's very pretty. I can see why you'd be smitten."

"Well, I did marry her." Caz tried to smile, but it felt off. She hadn't quite admitted to herself yet that she was, in fact, smitten. Was that even the word for how she felt about Grace? She had no clue and wasn't about to put any stock in it standing here. "Thanks again." She turned to walk away, then stopped and turned back. "Also, sorry about the vest and pants—not my best look." She nodded to them both before backtracking to where her own seat was.

"I cannot believe you did that," Grace said, her face

registering a weird mix of shock and awe. "What did you say?"

Taking her seat again, Caz pulled the linen napkin back in place across her lap and then picked up the menu. "Only that my wife had pointed out I was a nincompoop for not recognising her."

"A nincompoop?" Grace laughed loudly, quickly becoming aware that people were staring. "I can't believe you met her and had no clue."

"Well, I don't listen to classical music, do I?" She grinned. "Imagine your dad's face, though, if he came into the garage and that was playing."

Conversation was interrupted when the waiter appeared and took their order, but the moment he left, Grace sat up straight. "So..." she started, gaining Caz's attention. "I was thinking," Grace continued as Caz poured them both a glass of water from the carafe, "maybe it would just be easier using the clinic."

"Okay," Caz replied slowly. "What's brought about this change of mind?"

"It would just be easier wouldn't it, all round? Finding a donor, making sure all the tests are done? It would be easier for you, and us."

"Not gonna lie, I think it's the sensible option." Caz reached for her glass and took a mouthful of water, her mouth getting drier by the minute. Was it the topic of conversation, or the way Grace looked so happy in that moment, that she felt more for her than just being her friend? She *was* smitten, wasn't she?

Grace nodded. "I know, I just thought...I thought if it was you that did it then it would be like we really did make a baby together."

Caz smiled at the sentiment before reaching across the

table for her hand. "Whatever is meant to be will be, and if we are lucky enough to have a baby, it will be a baby we love, and that is all that matters. It won't matter how it got here."

"You're right." Grace squeezed her fingers.

"Hope I'm not interrupting," a voice to the left of Grace said. Alex stood beside her, smiling down at them holding hands. "It was lovely to meet you yesterday, Caz, and you must be Grace."

"Oh, yes. Hello." Grace gushed a little, and Caz held in the giggle that threatened to erupt. "Wow, I am such a fan, especially your last album."

"Ah, yes. *Euphoria* was a little different." She leaned down, glancing back at Morgan quickly. "It's amazing what the right kind of inspiration can create."

"Quite," Grace said, flashing a glance at Caz.

"And we were wondering if you would both like to join us later? We're just going to be enjoying the sunset around the firepit again. We'd love to share it with you both."

"Oh, that would be—"

"We'd love to," Caz cut in.

"Brilliant. No need to bring anything, Morgan never lets the supplies run low." Alex smiled at them both. "Well, I will leave you to your lunch. Around eight?"

"We will be there," Caz answered for them both, the look on Grace's face saying there wouldn't be any other answer that would be acceptable.

"Yes, definitely." Grace's grin widened as Alex made her way back to her own table. "Oh my God! We're going to Sasha's house to watch the sunset!"

CHAPTER THIRTY

"What shall I wear?" Grace said, rummaging through the sparse clothing choices she'd brought with her. They were only going away for a break, mostly lounging on the beach, making use of the balmy weather. She hadn't planned for a night at the home of a famous composer.

Caz grinned. "Considering my attire the other night was my vest and pants, I am pretty sure they won't be judging you on anything you choose tonight."

Grace considered that for a moment.

"Doesn't matter, I'm not you." She bent down and pulled another drawer open. "And you've told them about us, so they're already judging me."

"Wow, triggered much?" Caz chuckled and stood up.

Grace straightened and met her face to face. "No, I just… we're unconventional, I know that, but literally, these people are the only ones who know that."

"Right, and they invited us over to their place. I don't think anyone is judging us except maybe…you?"

"I'm not, I just…" Grace sighed, "I'm just used to us playing a couple and being all lovey-dovey around everyone and it feels weird not having to do that tonight, and now I am panicking about how to act and—"

Caz gripped Grace by the shoulders. "Just be you. That's all you ever have to do—just be you."

Their eyes met, both a little wet with emotion. It didn't go unnoticed by Caz when Grace's stare dropped to her mouth before quickly rectifying.

Caz smiled. "Just be you, alright?"

Grace nodded.

"And we'll just be us," Caz continued, releasing her grip on Grace. "If that means we're like a couple, then that's okay—that's who we are, okay?"

"Okay," Grace said quietly. She turned back to the wardrobe and picked out a cute white summer dress. Holding it up against herself, she looked in the mirror and found Caz staring at her. "What about this?"

"I think you look beautiful in whatever you wear, but yeah, that's nice. Shows off your tan." Caz smiled and looked away, but not before the blush hit her cheeks. What did it mean when Grace said, *"I'm just used to us playing a couple and being all lovey-dovey around everyone and it feels weird not having to do that tonight?"*

"What are you wearing?" Grace asked, interrupting Caz's thoughts from going any deeper.

Caz looked down at herself. Blue jeans and a T-shirt with a Mickey Mouse face on it. "This?" Grace frowned at her. "It's nicer than vest and pants!"

"Yes," Grace laughed, "maybe you're right." She turned back to the wardrobe. "We should pick up a bottle of wine or something."

"Alex said we didn't need to."

"It's still polite to take something, though," Grace said as she pulled off the top she'd worn earlier. In just her bra and shorts, she grabbed a towel. "Just need a quick shower."

As she walked away, Caz mumbled to herself, "So do I—a cold one."

CHAPTER THIRTY-ONE

Caz held the flowers up to her nose and sniffed them. "These are nice," she said as they both walked barefoot on the sand, shoes dangling from their free hands.

"Wow, is that their house?" Grace asked, as the wall of glass windows up ahead reflected the waning sun.

In daylight it would look even more impressive, she was sure.

"Yep, I think so." As they neared, the decking became more visible and the comfortable seating and firepit stood out. "Yep, that's it," Caz said, just as Morgan stepped out and waved at them.

"Hey," Morgan called out, a big smile on her face. She turned back to the door and shouted something through, presumably to Alex.

"Hi," Grace called back, hopping up the first step as Caz followed and held out the bouquet.

"Aw, those are beautiful, thank you," Morgan said, taking them from her just as Alex appeared. "Smell these." Morgan grinned, pushing the flowers into Alex's face.

Alex took them off of her and playfully slapped her. "Can you behave when we have guests?" she admonished, but the smile said something else; something warm, but with a slight undertone only Morgan read, because she blushed instantly and it didn't go unnoticed by Grace, who glanced quickly at Caz and smiled her own silent message.

Alex turned to their guests. "Thank you. These are lovely

and I have just the vase for them."

"Can I get you both a drink?" Morgan asked, looking at Caz and then Grace.

"Love one," Caz replied.

"Yes, why not?" Grace added, stepping a little closer to her wife, smiling when Morgan did.

"Grab a seat. I made some nibbles too," Morgan said a little excitedly. "Can you tell we don't have guests often?"

Alex smiled at her before she chimed in, "We don't get many guests, mainly because I prefer it that way."

"Unless you count Francine, who seems to come and go as she pleases lately." Morgan poked her tongue out at Alex. "Alex's manager," she explained. "Beer? Wine? Something less alcoholic?"

"Wine would be great," Grace said, before adding, "Caz prefers beer."

"Red? White?"

"Either...whatever is easiest," Grace gushed, not wanting to cause anyone a headache over a simple question. She really didn't mind.

Alex swept past Morgan. "Just open both, darling. I'll be right back." She held up the flowers with one hand and with the other, playfully slapped Morgan's backside. "Make yourselves comfortable," she said over her shoulder to their guests, laughing when Morgan's eyes narrowed and the grin appeared that said very much how she would be getting her own back later.

"Be right back," Morgan said.

With both of their hosts gone, Grace giggled. "Can you believe we're here?"

Caz sat down on a comfortable wicker sofa-style chair and grinned. Seeing Grace so happy always gave her tummy a tumble. She was beginning to realise that a lot lately. Had it always been the case and she'd just ignored it because Grace was in the friend zone all these years? Then she reminded herself Grace was still in the friend zone, wasn't she?

"They're just people," she said. Her own excitement was building, but not from being in the presence of a celebrity. Her excitement came from being with Grace, out with another couple; a couple very much at ease with each other, and around other people.

"Famous people," Grace exclaimed before she sat down beside Caz and leaned against her. "This is such a nice way to end our holiday."

"Honeymoon." Caz raised an arm up and allowed Grace to get more comfortable. "Yeah, it is," she said, just as Morgan came through the door with a tray in her hands and a quizzically playful look on her face when she caught sight of them. Caz pressed her lips together in an attempt not to smile, but it was a pointless exercise. She knew what it looked like, too.

"Here we go," Morgan said brightly, placing the tray down onto the table and handing out drinks. "Did I hear 'honeymoon'?"

Grace sat up and straightened, her back now against the sofa.

"Oh, don't move on our behalf." Morgan smiled, "One more of these and I'll be just as relaxed against my lover, too."

Caz stiffened and stared at her. The proverbial deer in the headlights look appearing on her features.

"It's okay, you don't have to pretend. Caz told me she explained our...situation to you both." Grace finished speaking just as Alex joined them. "And yes, technically a honeymoon..."

"Relationships of all kinds can work when two people love each other enough to recognise it," she said, taking a seat beside Morgan. Their hands instinctively reached for each other. "Ours isn't exactly what society would deem acceptable—getting married and still living in our own homes, but we like it that way."

"For now," Morgan added, "I'm here more than there."

"Yes, and I am getting used to that." Alex smiled and leaned into kiss her. "But when you finish a long night shift, the last thing you want is to have me plonking away on the piano."

"There are worse things to have to listen to." Morgan grinned, raised their hands, and kissed the back of Alex's.

"I thought I read you'd retired," Grace said.

"From the world, yes, but from music? Never." Alex grinned. "And I need that time, to just play."

"I can buy earplugs, or you can get a keyboard with headphones." Morgan grinned at the face Alex pulled.

"What a suggestion." Alex laughed. "I do love you being here, though. Maybe we should rethink it, after all." She looked at Caz and Grace. "Relationships evolve, don't they?"

To Caz's surprise, it was Grace who said, "Hopefully." She glanced quickly at Caz before lifting her glass and sipping. "Once we have a baby, everything will change, won't it?"

Caz breathed deeply, smiling slowly as she caught sight of Morgan staring at her. *Was she willing her on?*

"Having a baby will definitely mean changes. No more of this for a while," Caz joked, holding up her bottle of beer.

"You can still drink beer." Grace laughed and poked her.

"U-uh, if you can't, I can't."

Grace smiled and leaned in to kiss her cheek. "You're very

sweet."

"Remember that next time I piss you off."

They all laughed.

"Happen often?" Alex asked with a mischievous grin curving her lips.

Grace plucked her glass up from the table once more. "Not as often as you might think, but too often for my liking." She winked.

It didn't take Grace long to lose the inhibitions caused by sitting in the presence of someone as famous, or as rich, as Alex. Soon enough, she was bombarding her with questions about people she'd met and where she'd played. Caz just sat back and listened, enjoying the way Grace became so animated.

When Alex offered to play something for Grace, she'd leapt at the chance and the two of them went inside. Musical notes drifted out through the open door moments later.

"You should tell her," Morgan said, smiling at Caz. "Tell her how you feel about her."

Caz shook her head. "I can't, that wouldn't be fair."

"It's obvious she cares for you," Morgan continued. "I think you might be surprised—"

"Or I might ruin the only thing that has ever made any sense to me." Caz smiled sadly. "She's everything, and I won't risk losing what we have."

CHAPTER THIRTY-TWO

With Alex sat at the piano, Grace listened as she played through a piece. It was beautiful; up and down the scales Alex's fingers moved, creating such emotion, Grace couldn't avoid the feelings that swelled within her.

"I wrote this for Morgan when we were pretending we weren't together," Alex admitted. "I think those moments, at times, were so exciting, but daunting too."

"How so?" Grace asked.

"There were so many variables. This life I live isn't exactly…it can be hard for any partner of mine to be part of."

"So, what was it that made you go for it?"

Alex smiled up at her, the music changing into something gentler. "I realised that there was nobody on this Earth who got me like she did, and who allowed me to get her."

Grace considered it, her own thoughts moving to Caz and how she made her feel. "I can understand that."

"Do you love her?" Alex asked, still playing, but her eyes watched Grace's face.

Staring out of the window, Grace smiled at Caz talking animatedly with Morgan. She turned back to Alex. "Yes, she's my person."

"I think that's obvious to anyone who meets you both." Alex grinned. "But you're not attracted to her?"

"I'm straight. So, yeah, kind of an issue…"

"That's not what I asked." Alex smirked playfully. "I've

slept with many straight women."

Feeling her face flush, Grace bit her lip. "I just...sometimes I look at her and I wonder if we could...but then I think about the mechanics of it all and I'm not sure that's something that does it for me."

"You know it's not all scissoring and sitting on a face, right?" Alex laughed gently. "Sex is sex, Grace. How you do it and what gets you off are personal choices."

Grace nodded. "We kissed..."

"She said."

"Then she said we shouldn't do that anymore, but then she kissed me again this afternoon. I like that. I like cuddling and kissing her."

"But?" Alex stopped playing.

"We got into this with an arrangement, and things have changed a little between us, but...I don't want to risk losing what we do have by experimenting with something I'm not sure I can—I don't want to let her think it might and then it doesn't happen, and it ruins what we have. I can live without sex. I don't think I can live without her."

Now it was Alex who nodded. "Well, she already put a ring on it, so I guess you have all the time in the world to figure it out."

Grace laughed. "Yes, maybe...I just hope it's enough for her."

Alex looked out through the door, towards the decking where she could see Caz. "She looks at you like you're enough."

"She does," Grace admitted.

CHAPTER THIRTY-THREE

They'd barely been home for a few hours when Grace announced she had an appointment for the clinic later that week.

"It just seems prudent to get the process started, don't you think?" she said, as Caz pushed clothing into the washing machine.

"I guess."

"You don't sound too excited."

Caz stood up and twisted around to lean against the worktop. "I'm just trying to stay grounded, you know, in case—"

"In case it doesn't work and I'm a complete wreck?" Grace stepped forward, moving slowly until she was stood right in front of Caz. Her arms snaked around her wife's waist, and she sighed contentedly when Caz reciprocated.

"I just want to be ready for all outcomes," Caz answered, kissing the top of Grace's head, taking comfort from the familiar scent of her shampoo.

"We can wait, if that makes it easier, I don't mind—"

"No," Caz said firmly. She took hold of Grace's shoulders and stared down at her. "This is what we want, right? It's the reason we did this."

"Yeah, but it needs to be the right time, and I feel like I'm rushing you."

Caz shook her head. "We don't have time, that's the point,

isn't it? Ageing eggs!" She smiled ruefully. "You're right, we need to move forward and do this."

"I love you," Grace said. "You have always been my stability—my safe space."

The words hit Caz harder than she thought they would, piercing deeper inside and awakening the part of her she'd been trying to shut down, the part that wanted more from this.

"I know, back at ya." She let go of her grip on Grace, the movement making Grace step back and create space between them. "I was thinking I'd get this washing on and then give the house a quick hoover. You want to grab a bath?"

Grace smiled. "Might as well...one last relaxing evening before work tomorrow."

"Those houses won't sell themselves," Caz joked, turning away to open the drawer for washing liquids. She closed her eyes and swallowed down the need to just spurt out her feelings. "I'll bring you up a cup of tea."

Strong arms reached around her again, the warmth of Grace's body pressing against her back. Caz placed her hands over those clasped around her.

"You're the best."

"Nah, but I am doing my best." Caz squeezed her hands. "And I'll always do my best for you, and our family."

"I appreciate you so much," Grace said, laying her cheek against Caz's shoulder. "You know that, right?"

Caz nodded. "Yes. I do."

"Good. If you ever feel like you need more from me, you just have to say so, right?"

For a moment, Caz wasn't sure what she meant. Her mind moved quickly through the words again, but before she could come up with a response, Grace added, "If I'm not being supportive, or I'm nagging too much, you'll say so?"

Caz let go of the breath she'd been holding. "Yeah, but that's not going to happen." She shrugged. "We're best friends, we already know all this."

They stood still and silent for a moment and then, when it felt like it was becoming awkward, Caz released Grace's hands, and the movement allowed Grace to pull away, a cold draught filling the space between them.

"Okay, I'm going to go and get ready to meet the girls. You sure you'll be alright on your own? Don't you want to meet up with Dani?" Grace asked. A last-minute plan to go for a drink with her friends was in store for that evening.

"I might see if she wants to come over and watch a film. I'm not really in the mood for going out."

"Fair enough." Grace kissed her cheek, grinned, and then she turned and left the room, leaving Caz to slump against the counter. She pressed her finger and thumb into her eyes, puffed out her cheeks and breathed out.

"You can do this," she told herself. "You can do this."

CHAPTER THIRTY-FOUR

Grace slid into the booth at Banjo's and reached for the large gin and tonic she'd ordered. Pushing aside the floating sprig of rosemary with the straw, she took a long sip and giggled.

"You're drunk already," Cressida accused with an endearing grin on her face.

"I am not." Grace faked her disgust at such an accusation. "I've only had three. It will take at least another two before I'm calling Caz to rescue me."

"Ah, and how is the lovely Caz...still keeping you well-oiled under the bonnet?" Jane winked and everyone laughed at the not-so-subtle innuendo.

Grace pulled a face. "Trust me, I get my needs met," she said with all the belief that it was true, because it was, wasn't it? Caz was more than a sufficient partner.

"Oh...do tell. We're all dying to know if it really is all it's cracked up to be," Cressida chimed in.

"Yes, I've told Greg it's a possibility that if he doesn't pull his socks up I, too, might jump the late-bloomer train to Lesville," Sandra said, instantly blushing and sucking on her straw as all eyes turned to her.

"Trouble at mill?" Jane asked, and Grace was grateful for the conversation to steer away from her own sex life...or lack of it.

"No, not really, I just...don't you ever just look at them and think, 'Do I even fancy you?'"

Cressida shrugged. "I think that's just how relationships go...you spend all your time with someone and suddenly, you're seeing all their flaws—"

"Not me," Grace piped up, "Caz is wonderful."

"Well, that's because it's all fresh and you fancy the pants off each other still," Sandra said. "And let's face it, she's not difficult to look at."

"I know, she's adorable. And the best kisser," Grace admitted.

"Okay, so back on track... Lesbian lovers—are they all that?" Cressida smirked, and sat back gleefully awaiting the answer.

Downing the rest of her drink, Grace felt the effects of the previous two. "I would choose Caz over every other lover I've had...every time."

A waiter appeared, carrying a tray with another round of drinks. He handed them out, flirted with Cressida, and then left them to it.

"How did we get these?" Jane asked, knowing none of them had gone to the bar.

Cressida pointed to a QR code on the table. "I ordered them. Drink up."

The glasses raised and chinked against one another with a loud *"Cheers"*, and they all swallowed down a mouthful.

Before their glasses hit the table, Jane flicked open the camera app on her phone and zapped the QR code herself. "Might as well continue how we mean to go on."

At drink seven, Grace drew the line.

"I'm done..." she slurred, and pushed the glass away. "Should...get Caz to...pick me up." She leaned against Jane. "She's so good to me, and she's hot, so hot, right? I'm...so hot." She began to fan herself.

"It is warm in here," Jane agreed, watching as Grace picked up her phone and began typing out a text.

When she finished the text, Grace said, "Just going to get some air. Caz will be here in a minute." She nodded to herself. It would take less than five minutes to drive from home to Banjo's at this time of night.

Proud of herself, she could at least still walk without staggering. Grace giggled as she opened the restaurant door and stepped outside. An instant breeze blowing across her face was refreshing.

"Woo, that's better," she said to herself, leaning against the window.

"You alright?" a man's voice said, and she turned to look at him. He was nothing special, but probably the kind of guy who might have gotten her attention once upon a time.

She smiled. "Yes, just warm inside."

"Yeah." He pulled a packet of cigarettes from his pocket and opened it, offering one to Grace.

"No, don't smoke, thanks."

"I keep saying I'm going to give up and then..." He pulled one free and lit it. "You go out, have a few beers and—" He shrugged and laughed. "On your own?"

"No, with friends, I'm just waiting for my ride." An image of Caz came into her mind, and the idea of riding *her* brought an instant blush to Grace's cheeks. "Sorry, what?" she asked, realising he'd said something.

"I said, I can give you a ride, you know, if you fancy it." The wink wasn't necessary. It was clear what he was interested in.

Grace straightened up. "Oh, that's...no, I'm married," she said, holding up her hand as proof.

"I don't see any husband around looking out for you," he said, edging closer.

"That's because she has a wife. Now back the fuck off," Caz said from behind him. Ramrod straight, using her full height, but still managing to look cool and relaxed, Grace couldn't help but take her all in; hair tied back, a baggy light-blue hoodie with her hands tucked into the front pocket, grey cargo pants, and black boots.

"Jesus, that's so hot," Grace muttered under her breath.

He turned, cigarette between his lips, palms up in surrender.

"No harm in trying, eh?" He chuckled, but backed away.

Grace felt relief wash over her, and something else: Desire. That was the hottest thing she'd ever witnessed. *"Back the fuck off,"* echoed in her head and those words sent a spark, that rushed downwards to her clit and hit with a jolt, like nothing she'd felt before.

CHAPTER THIRTY-FIVE

The coming weeks had been busy. Both had returned to work, and Grace was on cloud nine now that they'd undertaken their second attempt. Everything was going smoothly. All they had to do was wait and then, hopefully, enjoy the outcome.

A healthy child was all either of them wanted. They'd used a different donor this time; it felt more prudent. This was not a cheap process, and Caz had been somewhat concerned that using a tried and tested, and failed, model probably wasn't the best way to go this time around.

Grace had arranged desk duties only at work for the next week and Caz was running around like her own personal butler at home, making sure she didn't lift a finger.

"Put that down," she'd ordered when she'd come back from the shops and found Grace attempting to dust the unit in the living room.

Waving the yellow cloth at her, Grace tutted, "It's hardly going to—"

"You heard what the doctor said," Caz reminded her, moving quickly to take the cloth from her hand and guide her back to the couch. "Sit. Lay. Sprawl, but no unnecessary movement."

"I don't think he meant that I couldn't—" Grace stopped speaking and smiled at the way Caz was glaring at her. "Okay, fine, I will do as I'm told." She sat herself down.

"Thank you. Now, do you want spag bol or a stir-fry for dinner?"

"Whatever is easiest," Grace said, before noticing the

raised brow. "Stir-fry would be lovely, thank you." She slid down the cushion and brought her feet up.

"Great, I'll get cooking then."

"Can I at least come and sit in the kitchen with you?" Grace batted her eyelashes theatrically.

"Come on then." Caz added an even more dramatic eyeroll to the scene. Then she smiled. "If you're a good girl, I'll even let you chop some veg."

"Ooh, promises, promises." Grace laughed, as she stood up and almost skipped out of the room. "You know, when the baby comes—"

"If," Caz reminded her, keeping both their feet on the ground. They were due to do a pregnancy test the next day, but there were no guarantees at this stage. Despite both of them being excited to find out, it was Caz who was holding them both firmly rooted to the ground.

Grace ignored her. "I don't want you doing everything. We're in this together."

"Yeah, and that means you do nine months and hard labour, and I'll do my share."

"Uh, can we please not put 'hard labour' out into the universe, thank you. Calm, easy, and gentle labour are my preferences."

Caz laughed. "Alright, princess." She pulled a chair out from under the table. "Sit."

"Caz?" Grace said, sitting down as she was told.

"Yeah?" Caz answered. She'd turned away and was lifting the shopping bag up onto the counter to empty it out.

"I...while you were out, I..." Grace stopped talking. The sound of something plastic and light tapped against the tabletop.

Caz turned slowly to see what she was not talking about and recognised the familiar object.

"I couldn't wait, and I thought, if I just find out then... either way, I could be prepared and—"

Putting the bag of onions down, Caz wiped her hands down her thighs, her eyes flicking back and forth between the woman she was married to and the pregnancy test lying flat on the table.

"I'm pregnant," Grace whispered, and then her mouth contorted and what should have been a smile, became something else.

"What...why...why are you crying?" Caz rushed towards her and fell to her knees in front of Grace.

"I'm just...I dunno...relieved, happy, but...I didn't think it would happen, and now it has, and..." Now Grace laughed, wiping her eyes, before she reached for Caz and pulled her close, kissing her cheek. "We're having a baby."

"We're having a baby?" Caz asked, and then as the words settled, she grew more confident. "We're having a baby!" She jumped up, hopping around the room like an idiot, whooping as Grace laughed at her. Finally, she stopped and returned back to her spot, kneeling on the floor. "We're having a baby."

"We are. We're going to be parents," Grace said, taking Caz's hand and bringing it to her stomach. "In here, is our baby."

CHAPTER THIRTY-SIX

The first thirteen weeks were the target. That was what the doctor at the clinic said when the pregnancy was confirmed. Get through those and they could start telling everyone their news. But right now, they still had eight more to go 'til they reached the relatively safe zone, and it felt like a lifetime away.

"Lunch," Caz said, handing Grace a perfectly packed cool bag with nothing but healthy, hearty food stuffs for her and the baby. "I've added some extra olives."

Grace's eyes lit up. The past two days she had developed a craving. The book said they shouldn't arrive before five weeks for most people, but apparently some got them from day one. *Olives don't seem too bad*, Caz had thought, until she found Grace dipping them into English Mustard.

"And yes, I added the mustard," she said when Grace looked imploringly at her. "Just make sure you eat them out of sight of anyone else. That little concoction will properly give the game away."

Coming around the table, Grace leaned up on tip-toes, not taking any chances by wearing heels and tripping. She was back to being shorter than Caz.

She kissed Caz's cheek just as Caz was about to spin around and remind her to drink more water.

Their mouths met. The kiss was soft and gentle. Nothing more.

Grace pulled away and smiled. "Thank you for being so considerate." She straightened her suit jacket and added, "Won't be fitting in these much longer." The grin she shared lit up her face. "I'll see you tonight,"

"Yep, phone me if you need anything," Caz called after her retreating form.

When the coast was clear, Caz reached tentatively and touched her lip. One simple kiss and it felt like fire had left a scorch mark. "Shit."

She grabbed her keys and wallet and followed Grace out of the house.

Dani shuffled around the car Caz was working on and leaned on the edge of the open bonnet. Gazing in, she tried to see what Caz was fiddling with, but none of it made much sense to her.

"Got no tyres to fit?" Caz said, not looking up as she twisted the tool half a turn and tightened the screw.

"Nope, otherwise, I wouldn't be standing here gawping at what you're doing, would I?" Dani said sarcastically, but with a playful enough grin. "Wanna go to the pub later?"

"Can't," Caz said. She wiped her hands on a rag and then placed the tool back in its slot.

Dani puffed her cheeks out.

"What?" Caz asked with her own sigh.

"Nothing." Dani shrugged. "It's just…been a while, you know, since we all went out and just got blathered."

"So, get Portia and Dalilah to go. They never turn down an opportunity to get drunk and hunt for girls."

"It's not the same. Three doesn't work the same as four, and anyway, it's you I wanted to hang out with."

Caz looked at the sorrowful face in front of her and felt a pang of guilt. The lies kept building, and she hated doing that to her friend, but what else could she do?

"Footy season starts soon. We can get to a game, right?" Caz offered.

"That's weeks away," Dani whined.

"It's two weeks." Caz laughed. "Everton women at home."

"Yeah, but—" Dani was cut off.

"I just…I can't right now. It's not the best time for me to be galivanting off." Caz smiled and felt it widen on her cheeks as she remembered the reason why it wasn't a good time. They were having a baby. Against all the odds, and despite her reticence, they were going to have a baby.

Dani's eyes narrowed. "What are you up to?"

"Nothing," Caz said quickly—too quickly.

For a moment, Dani considered things, and then her face scrunched up and she made an 'eww' sound. "Oh, God, keep your sex life to yourself."

"I didn't mention sex." Caz laughed. *If only,* she thought. "Grace and I are just…we've got a lot planned at the moment and I don't want to let her down."

"Quite right," the booming voice of their boss, and Grace's father, said from behind them. "My little Sweetpea deserves the best, doesn't she?"

Caz spun around and almost saluted him.

"Yep, and I am absolutely making sure that happens."

Ron chuckled. "'Course you are, never doubted it for one second. I see the way you look at her. I know that child of mine is as loved now as the day she was born."

Red cheeks burned as Caz looked away.

"No need to be shy about it." Ron laughed and slapped her on the back.

"Nah, not shy…" Caz shook her head and tried to smile, now imagining loving Grace in a far more intimate way than either of them had agreed to. "Which is why I need to be home on time," she said, looking at her watch and then tossing the oily rag onto the counter.

CHAPTER THIRTY-SEVEN

Caz got home before Grace. She ran upstairs and jumped into the shower, scrubbing the oil and grease away. With a towel wrapped around her, she twisted the taps on the bath and dumped a huge dollop of Grace's favourite bubbles. The scent of peach and vanilla instantly filled the air.

She'd done this a lot in the last couple of weeks, rushing home, having a warm bath ready, while she cooked dinner, and insisting that Grace rest, feet up and happy.

The weather was turning cooler as September edged towards October. Leaves were falling and skies were darkening, and the fire was lit most evenings. It was a cosy home, and that made it too easy to inch closer to each other.

Not that Caz was complaining.

If that was all she would ever have with Grace, she was good with it. She loved it even more when Grace would snuggle in, grab Caz's hand and pull it to lay against her stomach, and they'd talk about the future, what the baby might look like, and names.

Caz liked Gregory for a boy. Grace had said it was far too posh, but then she picked Amelia for a girl, which Caz liked, but pointed out so did almost every other parent on the market for a good moniker for their kid.

She pushed her hand into the water, checking the temperature as she swirled it to make more bubbles. Turning, she almost jumped out of her skin when Grace appeared in the doorway. Her arms moved so quickly that the towel almost fell away.

"Bloody hell, Grace." Caz laughed, readjusting the cotton covering around herself. "Scared the shit out of me."

"Language," Grace admonished playfully. "That's a pound in the swear jar, Madden."

They'd made a pact to never swear around the children. They'd agreed to never shout at each other, or the kids, if they could help it, and to always find kind words and ways to say things that wouldn't end up scarring their offspring for life.

"Sorry, my bad." She sagged a little. "Good day?"

"Yeah, got an offer on two different homes, so fingers crossed, I'll be hitting my bonus early this month, but I am glad its Sunday tomorrow. My back aches a little."

"That's great, about the houses, not your back. You're amazing." Caz grinned.

The way Grace's face lit up at the compliment gave Caz a thrill, and it was in that moment, she really understood something fundamental: She'd always loved Grace, like loved— really loved—not just a friendship love. It was real, deep, and connected love, that if she were honest, she'd never found with anyone else.

Her thoughts flicked back to Morgan telling her to just admit it to Grace.

But she couldn't.

She shook herself out of it and pushed it all back down again. There was no place for such things. They were not that kind of couple, no matter how much she might want them to be. Her eyes moved down and watched as Grace's hand rubbed gentle circles on her tummy—something she'd been subconsciously doing a lot lately.

"So, I've got dinner all planned. Chicken wrapped in prosciutto and stuffed with mozzarella, with a side of olives and mustard."

"Sounds perfect," Grace answered, her attention turning toward the bath. "For me, I assume?"

"You assume correctly. Jump in, take as long as you like,

and I'll bring you a cup of that horrible tea you love."

"It's not horrible, you just need a refined palate for it."

Caz grimaced and ducked past her.

"If you say so."

"I do say so," Grace called out after her.

Caz was already on the landing and smiling to herself as she headed into what was once her bedroom but now just housed her clothes.

"You are so under the thumb," she muttered happily. She yanked the drawer open and pulled out fresh underwear. Boxer-style shorts with the Bath Street Harriers logo on them that Dani had gotten her last Christmas in the secret Santa exchange. She again felt a pang of guilt that her friend was in the dark about everything, because she felt sure, when she could finally tell Dani and the others, nobody was going to be annoyed she was spending time at home.

And then she had to admit, she did kind of miss hanging out with the gang.

When she was dressed in matching sweatpants and hoodie, she skipped down the stairs. She was halfway when she stopped.

"Grace, do you need anything?"

There was no answer. So, she tried again, this time walking back up three stairs.

"Grace? I'm going to get dinner on."

A strangled mewling sound filtered out through the closed door, followed by a more stringent cry.

"Caz!"

Bolting up the remaining steps, and without thinking any further than getting there, Caz opened the door and rushed inside.

Grace was curled up on her side, one hip protruding from

the water, her left arm clinging to the side of the bath, with her face contorted, leaning against the edge.

"What's wrong?" Caz said, instantly dropping to the floor and getting as close as she could.

Eyes wet with tears, stared back at her.

"Grace? Talk to me."

She mouthed something so inaudible that Caz needed to lean closer still.

"Say that again."

This time, in a hushed whisper, she heard, "I'm bleeding."

There was a rush of adrenaline that moved its way like lightning through Caz's body, numbing any sense of pain or upset.

"A lot?" she asked, but her eyes already answered for her when she looked to the water and saw the murky colour beneath the fading bubbles.

Grace nodded.

"Okay, so, let's get you out of there and go get you and... let's get everything checked out, yeah?"

"What if—"

Caz stood up and grabbed a towel, holding it up. She closed her eyes and allowed Grace her dignity.

"Let's not focus on the negative, it might be completely normal, or just something we need to fix." She kept her voice as steady as she could, trying desperately to hold on to anything positive.

The sound of water cascading, and then the feel of Grace pulling the towel towards her meant she could open her eyes again.

"It's going to be okay, whatever happens, alright?"

Grace nodded, but the tears now trickling down her cheek

said otherwise when she doubled over in pain and cried out, "Caz, we can't lose—."

There was nothing Caz could say, other than offer Grace a hand and help her out of the bath. "Let's just get things checked, okay?"

CHAPTER THIRTY-EIGHT

It was the silence that hurt at first. The inability to speak and comfort one another with words. Caz had had her heart broken multiple times, but nothing felt as painful as this did, or what was about to come.

They'd lost a child.

This time, there had actually been a pregnancy, and now it was gone and both of them were hurting.

A shared dream, shattered into a million tiny heartbreaking pieces of grief and sadness and anger.

But in the midst of it all, they were losing each other, too.

The hospital had scanned and tested, confirming a miscarriage within minutes of them being seen. It had all felt so surreal—almost unbelievable, all so matter-of-fact, as though this happened to them every day.

Their baby had just stopped existing.

The nurses had been kind enough, but nothing could comfort Grace in that moment. Medication and a leaflet were organised, explaining everything they would need to do in the coming days and weeks.

The tissue, as they were now calling it, would leave the body in its own time, but the medication would speed up the process if Grace wanted to take it and not wait the ten to fourteen days it could take.

Grace followed the instructions the moment they were home and then went to bed with a hot water bottle against her stomach and her back turned. Caz stared up at the ceiling until Sunday drifted in, and they spent the entire day barely speaking, eating, or moving.

"You can't just go back to work, Grace," Caz had said Monday morning, when she'd woken from a fitful sleep to find Grace already dressed.

"Watch me," Grace said without looking at her. She shrugged on her suit jacket and fluffed her hair out from where it was stuck beneath the collar.

"But Grace, don't you think—"

Grace spun around. "I don't want to think, don't you get that? I want—I need to be busy—to not think. So get off my back and stop trying to mollycoddle me."

Caz felt the sting of tears erupt, but she forced them back down. "I'm not. I just think we should take some time and—"

"Process? Is that what you were going to suggest?" Grace stepped forward, teeth bared. "I don't need to process. Our baby died. That's all there is to it."

When Caz reached for her, Grace shrugged her off.

"Don't," she warned.

Caz sagged. "Grace, don't be like that."

"Like what?" Grace said, spinning around to glare at her. "I don't want you to touch me, okay? And you can move back into your own room." She grabbed her bag and stormed out of the lounge.

Caz listened as Grace paused to grab her coat and put her shoes on, and then the slam of the door closing made her jump out of her skin.

"I lost the baby too, Grace," she screamed, the tears finally bursting forth. "I lost a baby too," she repeated, as she fell to the couch and grabbed a cushion, pushing it against her face to muffle the sound of her sobbing.

Her phone buzzed and she ignored it, too lost in her own world of upset and hurt. She needed to do this now, or she might never. Caz Madden wasn't known for her emotional outbursts, unless they were in defence of someone she loved—like Grace.

When the phone buzzed again, she wiped her eyes and picked it up. A blurry text from Dani swam into her vision:

Dani: Get moving, you're late.

Followed by another one:

Dani: Too late, Ron's noticed. Say you had a flat tyre, that's what I've told him.

Caz groaned. The last thing she wanted to do was go to work. But what else could she do when her boss was her father-in-law and didn't know his daughter had been pregnant?

Caz: Overslept. Be in soon. Thanks for covering.

She got up and dragged herself up the stairs to the bathroom, where she washed her face and stared at herself in the mirror.

"It'll be alright. She's just upset...she doesn't mean what she's saying," she said to herself, closing her eyes to stop the next trickle of tears from escaping. Her eyes were bloodshot and swollen.

They'd spent most of the night crying silently together, and Caz had thought that was a good sign—that they'd get through it all together. She hadn't expected the sudden coldness from Grace.

She rooted through the cupboard for that little pot of stuff Grace used whenever she complained about looking puffy, It wasn't there.

"Fuck."

CHAPTER THIRTY-NINE

Rather than drive in and have to lie, she left the car at home and took the bus, walking the last part of the journey. It had done her good; allowed her more opportunity to process everything and work through her sadness before she was faced with interacting with people.

Dani spotted her instantly. She was on the phone and couldn't leave the office, but Caz could feel the eyes on her the entire way as she walked through the garage and found her toolbox.

She already knew what she was doing: Finishing off the Ford Focus she'd started the day before. New brakes, pads, and tracking; all simple enough if she could just get focused and get her head into it.

Checking it was safe, she hit the button that would raise the car up so she could get underneath it and crack on. Work would be her solace today, too.

But she should have known that small bit of peace wouldn't last long.

"Car sorted?" Ron said. He'd bent over to look under the car at her.

"Nah, I walked in," she said, not turning to look at him and lie to his face. "I'll fix it later."

"Well, we'll say no more about it, but next time, make sure you call in. I don't want them lot thinking you get special treatment just cos we're family."

"Sure. Sorry, Ron," she said. Her hand squeezed the wrench a little harder as she twisted a bolt. "I'll make up time in my—"

"Give over, will ya. Like I said, just call, or get Grace to call. In fact, that would be nice, she's been quiet lately. Everything alright?"

Caz stiffened.

Grace had been quiet with everyone. She was too excited about the baby to see people and not blurt it out, so she'd just been keeping out of the way, waiting for the time when it would be safe to shout it from the rooftops. That wouldn't happen now, though, would it?

"Yeah, you know, just the usual stuff people get busy with. I'll tell her, though…to call you."

"Alright, well, I'll leave you to it then." He walked away and Caz got back to it.

She twisted the wrench and it slipped off the bolt, her knuckle scraping across metal. "Fuck," she hissed to herself before sucking the sore spot.

"Not your day, is it?" Dani grinned as she poked her head under. "You alright? You look like shit."

"Thanks."

"Seriously, are you alright?" Dani moved closer, concern written all over her face. "You look like shit."

Ignoring the insult, Caz said, "I'm fine, yes. Just—"

"Had a row?"

Caz nodded. "Something like that."

Someone turned the radio up and started singing along to one of the songs, making both women turn to watch for a moment.

"If you want to chat about it…" Dani said with a shrug. "I'm available."

"I don't, but thanks," Caz responded. "It's…there's nothing to say about it right now. Just got to work things out with Grace and then it will be fine."

Dani looked at her as though she could see right to her core. "Must be serious…"

Caz rubbed her hand over her face and sighed deeply. "Can we change the subject?"

"Sure…just…never seen you like this before. I didn't think you two ever argued—"

The wrench landed on the floor.

"For fuck's sake, Dani, please…just drop it, alright?"

Dani's hands raised instantly as she stepped back and away from poking the bear any further.

"I'll get us a cuppa, okay?"

Caz nodded, bent down and grabbed the tool.

"Okay, thanks. And sorry…I didn't mean to shout."

"It's alright."

She'd composed herself by the time Dani reappeared carrying two cups of steaming tea. She handed one to Caz and placed her own down on top of the toolbox, producing a packet of chocolate Hobnobs from her overalls' pocket.

"Figured a few of these wouldn't hurt," she said, with a smile that said she was unsure of anything she might say right now.

Caz took one and bit into it.

"I'll be fine," she said, mostly to herself than to Dani. "All couples argue." *Except we're not a couple and this is bigger than any argument ever could be,* she thought to herself.

"Yeah, they do…but…" Dani scrunched up her mouth as she contemplated whether to say it or not. "You don't cry about it, and you look like…well, you looked like you did, and I hate seeing you upset, because I ain't used to it, and I don't even know what to do or say to—"

Caz pressed her thumb and forefinger into her eyes and relieved the pressure.

"Just make tea...and bring biscuits." Caz smiled sadly.

They stood in silence and drank their tea, nibbling on the odd biscuit here and there, until Caz's phone broke through with a buzzing noise from her pocket.

Putting her cup down, she pulled it free and noticed it was Grace's office number, and a small thrill ran through her. If Grace was calling, then it had to be a good sign, right?

"Grace, hi," she said, answering the call instantly and then turning away and walking towards the other side of the car for privacy. Because if Grace had called to give her an earful, she didn't need everyone listening in.

"Hi, Caz, it's Pete, listen...Grace is...well, she's told us about what's happened."

"Right."

"We're obviously very sorry for your loss and we're insisting she goes home, but to be honest, I don't think she's in any fit state to drive."

Caz was already heading up the stairs to Ron's office. "I'm on my way. I don't have my car, though, so I'll have to cadge a lift or get a cab, but I'm coming."

"Okay, we can deal with things this end."

"Right, so you won't let her leave or do anything—" What was she even suggesting? Things were not that bad, where they?

"Don't worry and don't rush." Pete lowered his voice and said, "She's safe, she's just upset and she needs you."

"I'm not sure how true that is, but...I'll be there asap." She closed the call and rapped her knuckles on Ron's door, opening it without answer. "I need to go."

He sat back in his chair and stared at her. "Why?"

"Because..." She swallowed, worrying her bottom lip with her teeth as she considered what to tell him. "Grace isn't feeling well and her manager just called to ask me to come and pick her up."

Now, Ron sat up, paying attention. "Well, what are you waiting for? Get going."

"I…I don't have my car, and I'll need to drive Grace's when I get there…can you call me a taxi?"

"No," he said, standing up and moving towards the door. He leaned out. "Dani?" When she looked up at him and mouthed, 'What', he shouted down, "Get the van and take Caz here and drop her off at Grace's office."

"I can get a cab. I've wasted enough of your time today—" She felt the tears beginning again and sniffed, gulping in air and swallowing down the emotions.

Ron closed the door with as slow and quiet a movement as Caz had ever seen from him.

"I don't know what's going on with you two, but I can see quite clearly that sommat is up. Now, I'm not going to pry, because I would like to think you'll both tell me in your own time if it's something I need to know about. But in the meantime, whatever it is, it needs fixing." He placed a warm palm on her shoulder. "So, you go home, and you and my Sweetpea will work this out. Because I've never seen her as happy as she is with you."

Caz nodded. "I'll try."

CHAPTER FORTY

The van was a melting pot of stuff that didn't need to be there, empty Coke cans scrunched up in the door pockets beside half-eaten crisp packets and old newspapers.

"Who even reads newspapers anymore?" Caz said when she'd adjusted her seatbelt. Small talk or silence, those were her options for this trip.

"It's Jez. He's always got to have one, for the horses or something. I told him to just download an app, but you know Jez," Dani responded, understanding the mission without the need for instructions.

Caz stared out of the window.

It wasn't a long journey to the next town over where Grace's office was. As Dani turned into the high street, Caz could see the building up ahead, and the anxious feeling that had settled these past twelve hours or so, began to rumble around more loudly within her again.

A million questions flooded her brain, and for a moment, she was almost overwhelmed by it all. But then she stopped and reminded herself this wasn't about her. It was about Grace, and about grief. They'd either make it through or they wouldn't, but if they failed, it wouldn't be because Caz fell apart or gave up.

"Here you go," Dani said. She'd pulled the van into the kerb and Caz hadn't even noticed. "Look, I get it, you're not ready to talk about it…but when you are, I'm here, okay?"

Caz smiled a tight smile that stretched her lips more than her cheeks. "Thanks," was all she managed before she pulled on the lever and opened the van's big heavy door and jumped out.

She didn't look back, focused on one thing and one thing

only: Grace.

The door opened before she reached for it.

Tall, distinguished, hair mostly grey, and male, his smile was warm and sincere. "Hi, Caz. She's through the back with Reeja."

"Thanks, Pete," Caz said, stepping inside. She didn't politely wait to be shown through. Instead, she marched ahead, into the small corridor at the back that lead down to a small kitchen area with seating.

Her heart cracked another fissure when she saw the sight of Grace. Sitting at the table, arms folded in her lap, make-up streaked down her face, looking blank and numb.

"Grace?" Caz said gently. She nodded to the woman who had been sitting with Grace, who now stood up and moved out of the way.

"I'll leave you both," she said and squeezed Caz's bicep as she passed.

Squatting down, Caz took action. She reached for Grace's hand, and feeling no movement to stop her, she gripped it more firmly, lovingly rubbing her thumb over the back of Grace's fingers. "Hey." She tried a smile again when Grace turned and focused on her just enough. "Was thinking we should go home, yeah?"

There was a packet of wet wipes on the table and Caz pulled one free. Tentatively, she began to wipe away the smudged mascara and foundation until it was virtually all gone.

Grace said nothing, but when Caz pulled gently on her hand, she allowed herself to be drawn to her feet. Her bag and coat were on the table and Caz took them, one arm slipping around Grace as they inched towards the door and the back entrance where Caz knew Grace's car would be parked.

"Caz?"

The simple word—her name—said so sadly it almost

broke her, but she held firm.

"Yeah?"

"It's gone."

It took a moment for Caz to remember: The tissue—their baby.

Grace was still talking. "…the toilet, and I had so much pain I thought I'd faint and then, I felt it leave my body, and I couldn't—"

Caz put her arm around her, grateful not to be pushed away this time. They needed each other, didn't they?

"Let's go home, eh?"

"I don't want to go home."

Caz opened the back door. Daylight flooded in and almost blinded them both.

"Okay, we can go somewhere else," Caz said. She wasn't going to argue. Finding the keys, she hit the button and the alarm beeped. "Let's get into the car, and then we can decide what to do, yeah?"

Grace didn't agree or argue. She just complied and sat herself in the passenger seat. Caz all but ran around the car to the driver's side, jumping in and closing the door, and closing out the world outside.

"Do you need—" She stopped talking, leaned over and grabbed the seatbelt, yanking it too hard and it stuck. She calmed herself, released it, and tried again. This time when she pulled it, it came loose and she could clip it into the lock, making Grace as safe as she could be. "So, I thought we could just drive out to the coast…"

Grace didn't answer. She just stared absently out through the window, a solitary tear running down her cheek as though it, too, was trying to escape the sadness that was upon her.

The engine started and she pulled away just as the radio came on, the DJ waffling along to the end of one song before launching into the next. Caz turned it down and then thought better of it, and turned it back up just enough so the silence didn't feel quite so oppressive.

She took turn after turn until she was on the motorway and cruising towards the sea, clear skies up ahead.

Caz hoped that boded well.

"I think it would be good if we can talk," Caz said once the car had hit the right speed and she was able to just follow the road without needing to keep indicating and moving.

She didn't think Grace was going to answer, but then she heard. "What's to talk about?"

Caz glanced quickly across at Grace. She was still staring blankly out of the window.

"You know…just talk for now, and then…later, when we're ready—"

Now Grace turned to her, a look of incandescent fury in her eyes.

"Small talk? You want to fill the air with nonsense? Okay, fine, how was your day?"

Caz let out a deep breath, biting down the urge to fire back.

"That's not what I meant, but it's a start, and yes, it's better than this silence…this coldness you're throwing at me."

"I'm not throwing it at you," Grace said angrily.

"Yes you are. It's like you blame me."

Grace scoffed and folded her arms tightly over her chest. "Oh, make it all about you. Good one, Caroline."

"I'm not making it about me, I'm trying to engage with you so we can talk it out, but all I'm getting is anger and—"

"Maybe…just maybe, I *am* angry! Have you considered that?"

Indicating, Caz pulled the car off the motorway at the

next junction and drove down a country lane, the silence now palpable. When she spotted a layby, she stopped the car, unbuckled her seatbelt, and turned in her seat to face Grace.

"I have considered that. I'm angry too—at the world and the universe, but not you," Caz said. She felt her eyes moisten instantly. "I'm not angry or upset with you. I want to be there. I want to support you and for us to be a team, but you're pushing me away, and I don't understand why? It feels like you blame me… Did I do something wrong?"

"No. Of course not. I just…it's like there's a volcano in my chest and it's erupting, and I can't…I can't stop it, and I can't breathe, and nothing makes it any better…I…" She finally looked at Caz. "Why me? Why can't we do this? Why us?"

Caz shrugged. "Why not us? It's just how it is, it's not personal…we didn't do anything wrong, or hurt anyone…this just—"

"Our baby died," Grace whimpered. "Our baby, nobody else's, and maybe I am selfish and maybe I don't care about anyone else right now. That was our baby."

Tears streamed freely down their cheeks.

"I know. And you've every right to be angry and sad. Just… let me be angry and sad with you."

Hands reached for one another and the moment they connected, the tears became sobs for them both. Caz pressed the release button on Grace's seatbelt and pulled her into her arms.

"I've got you."

CHAPTER FORTY-ONE

The drive home didn't feel as long now. It was still silent in the car, but the oppressive cold shoulder had lifted and it was a more comfortable silence.

An acceptance.

Caz usually reversed onto the drive, but today it didn't seem to matter how easy it was to get off the drive in the morning. She'd already decided neither of them were leaving the house for work.

"Come on, let's get inside. I'll make us a hot drink and we can just—"

Grace stopped walking, her eyes leading Caz to follow her gaze and stop talking. Gertie was swinging, hands gripping the ropes as her legs shot out in front and her little body flew back and forth through the air, in rhythm with her screams echoing her delight.

Caz put her arm around Grace and led her towards the house.

"That should have been us," Grace whispered as Caz pushed the key into the lock and turned it.

"I know."

What else could she say? She didn't want to offer meaningless platitudes or promises of things she wasn't sure they could keep. There wasn't anything she could say to make it better. Every thought just felt so trite.

So she said the most British thing she could think of, "Let's get the kettle on, eh?"

Making herself busy, Caz filled the kettle and flicked it on. From her peripheral view, she could see Grace pulling off her suit jacket and untying her hair. Even in the depths of despair and distress, she looked beautiful, and Caz mentally slapped herself for thinking so. It wasn't the time for that, was it?

"Did you want tea or coffee?"

Grace stared at her. "I don't mind."

"Alright," Caz smiled, taking the lead, "tea it is."

She pulled down the caddy from the cupboard and spooned three heaped scoops into the pot, ignoring the fact she hadn't warmed it first. When the kettle boiled and hissed, she poured the water in, gave it a quick stir, and popped the lid on.

"Are you hungry?" she asked, attempting to stay as upbeat as she could. She wouldn't let Grace fall into the misery she'd suffered at Christmas. Grieving was something they'd do together this time.

"Not really," Grace answered, with no real interest in the question.

"What about—" Caz was turning, carrying the teapot and two cups in her hands.

"You should probably just move out now," Grace said, looking up at her, expressionless.

Caz halted.

She replayed those words over in her head to make sure she'd heard right and then continued forward. She put the teapot and the cups down and proceeded to pour.

"Why would I do that?" Caz asked calmly, pulling the chair out and sitting to the side of Grace.

Grace sighed.

"I don't understand the logic. Why would I leave? This is my home. We're committed to—"

"That was before," Grace interrupted.

Caz frowned. "Before what?"

"Look, we got into this because we both agreed we wanted a baby, and I can't...I can't give you that, so...you should leave and go and find—"

"Wait, what?" Caz reached out, her fingertips touching Grace's arm lightly. "You think... No, we didn't do this just because we wanted a baby, Grace!" She turned away, her emotions tumbling around like a washer on spin. She couldn't hold it in any longer, not now. She stood up, spun back around, and stared at Grace, eyes intense and brooding as she finally admitted the truth, "We did this because neither one of us knew how to ask for what we really wanted..."

Now it was Grace who frowned. "I don't know what you're talking about."

"Yes, you do." She stared at Grace so hard it forced her to look away. "You know, Grace."

"I don't...we...this was an arrangement...to have a baby."

"Was it? Maybe that's what we told ourselves when it started," Caz said. She had nothing to lose, except for everything, and if that was to be the case, she was going to go down fighting, so she took her seat again and calmed herself.

Grace narrowed her eyes. "What are you talking about?"

Caz smiled as she continued to look at her. "We love each other, and it was too big of a risk to admit to feelings and attraction, so we found a way to make it alright."

"Are you mad?" Grace scoffed. "We did this to have a family, not because—"

Caz shook her head and continued, despite the hot flush she was starting to feel in her cheeks and on the back of her neck as she interrupted, "And now that's maybe not an option and we're going to have to face the reality of what we really are."

"And what reality is that? Seriously, Caroline, I'm all ears."

"Don't do that," Caz said, pushing her chair back and standing up again. Turning away, she ran her hands through her hair. "Don't push me away because you're upset and hurting. I'm hurting too." Twisting around, she stared down at Grace and finally said what she'd wanted to say for months now, "I love you...and I know you love me."

"So?" Grace shook her head at her. "We've never denied that; all friends love each other."

"Yeah, they do...but this is different."

"I'm not gay!" Grace said, standing up, hands firmly on her hips. "That's just ridic—"

"Friends don't kiss each other, Grace," Caz interrupted.

She watched Grace's cheeks burn a fierce pink as she sat back down and said, "You didn't complain."

"Neither did you," Caz threw back at her before adding, "Friends don't marry each other either, Grace."

"You agreed to that—" Her hands were thrown up into the air in frustration.

"Yeah, I did. I got swept up in it all. I told myself it was exactly what I needed, and I was right, you—"

"So, wait," Grace glared, "you've had feelings for me this entire time and you just what, thought I'd come around? That's pretty shit, Caz."

"No, that's not it." Caz shook her head furiously. "I didn't know I had these feelings. I thought you and me were so friend-zoned that that wasn't ever an option, but then...being around you all the time, living with you, being your partner, supporting each other...hugging...sleeping in the same bed, the kisses—I started to realise I *could* love you in that way, and that it was okay to love you, and...I've felt that there's a part of you that feels the same way about me."

Grace stood up. "Don't be ridiculous."

"I'm not being ridiculous!" Caz shouted. "Why do you think everybody we know believed us so easily when we said we were getting married?"

"I don't know...what does it matter? Maybe we're just good liars."

"Bullshit," Caz said again. "That's bull and you know it. They believed us because they all saw it...long before we did."

"They saw what they wanted to see. I don't love you." Grace shook her head. "Not like that."

The words stung and Caz felt them hit hard and deep, Grace puncturing her heart in a way nobody ever had before.

Grace walked away towards the door, where she stopped and looked back at Caz before she said, "We should get a divorce."

CHAPTER FORTY-TWO

Caz left it a moment before she followed Grace out of the room and took the stairs two at a time. There was the sound of movement in their bedroom and she hovered outside trying to decide what her next move should be.

Grace was upset, obviously. They both were, but she couldn't just give up and let Grace make decisions for them both, decisions she felt sure they'd both regret if they went through with it.

Grasping the handle to the door, she pushed it open and stepped inside. Grace was moving all of Caz's things from drawers and shelves. It was all stacked neatly on the bed.

"We're not getting divorced, Grace."

Without stopping what she was doing or looking at her, Grace said, "I think it's for the best."

"You're not thinking straight, and you don't get to think for me—that's not fair."

"You can meet someone who can give you what you want," she said, still not stopping what she was doing, or looking at Caz at all.

"I already have that," Caz replied. She chewed her thumbnail as she watched the scene in front of her, her stomach roiling and she felt nausea building. This wasn't the way things ended between them.

"It was never going to work, let's face it, Caz." Grace finally looked at her. She held one of Caz's T-shirts in her hand for a moment before she slowly added it to the pile. "Especially now, if you have…feelings. It's for the best."

"Bullshit." The outburst caught them both by surprise. "Sorry, I just—I'm not leaving," Caz said with more firmness to her words. "There's more to us than that."

"Really? Like what? We can still be friends, Caz. In fact, it will be like nothing ever happened."

"That's ridiculous and so far from the reality of—"

"Of what?"

"Us…me and you. How we feel about each other."

Grace sighed. "You're my best friend and always will be."

"Tell me you don't feel it."

"Feel what?"

Caz rolled her eyes and sighed. "Don't play dumb, it doesn't suit you." She straightened up—chin out, chest forward. "Tell me you don't feel the same way."

Grace stared at her, the realisation of what Caz was asking now dawned on her and played out on her face.

"I can't have this conversation with you," Grace said, her voice shaking as she turned her back and continued with what she was doing.

Caz let her.

She watched every move until there was nothing of Caz's left off the pile. Stepping forward, Caz reached down and scooped it all up in her arms.

"I'll sleep in the other room if that's what you want, but we are having this conversation when you're ready."

Pressing her lips together, Grace remained silent and stubbornly refused to engage further, but their eyes locked and held until Caz twisted away and walked out of the room and down the hall.

Once inside what was now the spare room, she dropped everything onto the bed and let out a long, deep sigh.

"I'll show you, Grace Hart." She flopped down onto the mattress that she hadn't slept on for months. "You love me, I know it," she whispered to herself. "I know it."

It took just a few minutes to put her things away and make the bed up. She didn't need to glance at her watch to know that it was time for dinner. Her stomach told her it was with its constant rumbling. She wasn't even sure if she could eat, but she'd try. Life had to resume, didn't it?

Grace was still in her room. That much was clear by the silence in the rest of the house.

"I'm making dinner," Caz called out, and didn't wait for a response. She jogged down the stairs as fast as her socked feet would allow without slipping and breaking her neck. Because, then, who would look after Grace?

Opening the fridge, she found a less than attractive menu on display. *They really needed to go shopping*, she thought, before delving lower and into the freezer. There was a pizza and garlic bread. "That'll do."

By the time it was cooked, Grace still hadn't appeared. Standing at the bottom of the stairs, Caz shouted up, "Dinner's ready."

She mooched back to the kitchen and flicked the kettle on. Half a dozen lagers would be preferable to tea, but getting drunk wasn't going to earn her any brownie points.

The sound of shuffling feet behind her made her turn. Grace smiled sadly and slid onto a kitchen chair, pyjamas on, hair tied in a messy bun, make-up removed.

"Hey," Caz said, trying to sound upbeat, despite the hurt they were both feeling.

"Hey," Grace responded with no real enthusiasm.

Sliding a mug in front of Grace, Caz said, "Tea, unless you wanted something else?"

Grace reached for the mug, slid two fingers through the handle and wrapped her hand around it. "No, tea is fine. Thank you."

"It's just pizza and—"

"It's fine, I'm not really hungry."

CHAPTER FORTY-THREE

Grace picked at the crust of the one slice of pizza Caz had put on her plate, despite repeating that she wasn't hungry.

She could feel the way Caz was staring at her from across the table. Strangely, it didn't feel uncomfortable. There was an intensity there, sure, but it was Grace who felt awkward, because she knew there was some truth to what Caz had said.

She'd be a liar if she tried to say otherwise, and yet, she couldn't quite find the words to agree with the statement completely. So they sat in silence while she picked at the ham on her pizza and Caz breathed calmly, staring, and then quietly chewing anytime she took another bite.

It also didn't help the situation that Grace felt so guilty, about everything.

This had all been her idea.

Now there was a marriage, a best friend who was hurting, and no baby. And the one thing that linked them all, was herself.

She was the cause of all of it.

"Grace?" Caz's voice broke her from her thoughts.

"Sorry, what?" she said, finally looking at her with more than just a cursory glance like she'd been doing the entire time they'd sat here.

Caz smiled tightly. "I said, can you please try and eat something?"

"Oh," Grace managed, pushing the plate away, "I can't... I'm just..." Eyes wet with emotion, she blinked away the impending tears. "I'm sorry..."

"It's fine." Caz piled the piece back on top of the serving plate and stood up, carrying the remains of their meal to the counter. "There's some soup...I can heat that up if you'd prefer?"

Grace shook her head. "No, I really can't eat just yet, but... thank you for trying to take care of me." *For loving me*, she thought, too.

Caz pulled a drawer open and took out a roll of cling film to cover the food with. "That's my job, I'm your...best friend."

The choice of words surprised Grace. She was expecting, *"I'm your wife"*, and when it didn't come, she realised...it stung.

Maybe that was what she deserved. She'd tied her best friend down in a marriage so they would have a baby and she couldn't even do that right. And when Caz had shared her feelings, what had she done then? Pushed her away and told her she was ridiculous, when the truth was...she wasn't.

"Grace." Caz's voice broke as she turned and noticed Grace was crying.

She moved to her, squatting down at Grace's feet, hands instantly reaching for her.

"I don't want you to leave," Grace sobbed, "I can't..."

"I know." Tears pricked at Caz's eyes before they built and spilled over, rolling down her cheeks like hot lava. "I'm not going anywhere."

"Why? This isn't...I can't give you—"

Caz pulled her sleeve over her hand and wiped away Grace's tears. "It doesn't matter. I thought you felt the same way, but if you don't that's fine—"

Grace took her hand and held it, gazing into her eyes. "I can't give you a baby."

"Then that's just what's meant to be, and we can look at other options, or just..." She swallowed hard, her gaze dropping to Grace's mouth before rising back to her eyes again. "Nothing has to change."

Grace touched Caz's cheek gently. "Everything has to change, Caz."

"It doesn't have to."

"I love you so much, but I'm not gay."

CHAPTER FORTY-FOUR

"How are you feeling?" Caz asked.

She'd come upstairs to find Grace sobbing on the floor of the nursery. Little pink and blue teddies on the floor with her, except for one, the biggest, that Grace was clutching to her chest and almost screaming into.

Caz had dropped to the floor, wrapping herself around Grace from behind and holding her until the sobs died down. It was probably what she needed, maybe what they both needed, because Grace had calmed after that and allowed herself to be taken to bed. She'd lain there quietly while Caz had run down and brought the plate of leftover food upstairs, insisting they should try to eat something.

The room was warm as the rain lashed against the window outside; a dark and thunderous storm, but at least it was calm again inside the house.

Beneath the duvet, Caz lay prone, while Grace snuggled into her side. One of her arms wrapped around Caz's waist, her fingertips flexing and relaxing against the warm torso. Caz's arm was squashed beneath Grace, hooked around her shoulders, pulling her closer, but she wouldn't complain when it went numb and pins and needles crept in.

Remnants of pizza crusts and garlic bread on a plate rested on Caz's legs. She was grateful Grace had finally eaten something, even if it had just been a couple of half-eaten slices. It was better than nothing.

Grace sniffed and said, "I don't know...I'm still sad, but...

less angry?"

"That's good, I think." Caz squeezed her arm a little tighter. "You needed to be angry, and now, you can be sad."

"I don't want to be sad forever, but...it feels like I might."

"I'm not going to let that happen," Caz promised.

"Promise?"

"'Course, I've never failed you before, have I?"

For a moment Grace was quiet, but then she said, "No."

"Feels like there's a but there..."

Grace breathed in and out deeply. "I'm worried...that I'll fail you." Caz went to speak but Grace moved a finger to her lips. "Let me finish...please."

"Okay."

"I said that I loved you, and I do, not just as a friend. I find myself feeling things for you I've only ever felt with men before, but I'm not gay...I don't know what to do with that? Or how it works with you..."

"I get that...I'm kind of nervous too," Caz said. She reached for the plate and placed it down to the floor before twisting so she could face Grace. "I think right now isn't the time to worry about labels and whether you're gay or not."

Grace nodded.

"And I think maybe it would work better if we just let whatever it is between us happen in its own time. What does Dani say? Things should be organic?"

Grace chuckled. "Yeah, I like that idea."

"We've got all the time in the world. You already married me. So you can't escape." Caz smiled and pressed her lips against Grace's forehead.

"I like it when you do that."

"Kiss your head?" Caz questioned.

Grace nodded again. "My forehead, head...mouth," she said, looking up into Caz's eyes. "I think that time when you were drunk and kissed me...it was more than nice, but I just put it to one side and figured..." She laughed. "Oh, I dunno what I thought, but I knew I wasn't gay and so I didn't think about it again."

Caz drew her fingertip down Grace's cheek. "It's good to hear you laugh. See, I told you I wouldn't let you stay sad for long."

Eyes welled up instantly. "I know, and I know my emotions are all over the place."

"All totally normal under the circumstances."

"Yeah. Will you stay in here tonight?"

Caz chuckled. "You threw me out."

"I know, that was so mean, I didn't want to...I just...I couldn't see how we moved forward, and I didn't want to hold you back."

"You could never do that."

"And I took my anger out on you and I'm ashamed of myself for doing that." Grace looked away.

With one finger under Grace's chin, Caz brought her back, face to face. "It's okay, don't carry that..."

"Does that mean...will you move back in here?"

"I'm already here." She kissed her forehead again. "And I told you before, I'm not leaving."

CHAPTER FORTY-FIVE

"Do you think this is weird?" Grace asked Caz over breakfast.

"Gonna have to enlighten me...I've not had a cup of tea yet."

Grace smiled at her. It was something she'd been managing more often these past few days, locked away from the world outside where it was just the two of them.

"Okay...we're...backwards."

Caz lifted the teapot and poured a cup for herself and then topped up Grace's mug. "In what way?"

"Most people meet someone, find them attractive enough to start seeing them, then they sleep together, and then they fall in love and possibly get married."

"I see where you're going with this." Caz grinned and blew across the top of her cup of tea to cool it.

"Exactly, we're backwards. We got married, realised we love each other, and now we understand we're attracted to each other in a way neither of us thought about before."

"Let's go on a date, then. An official one. When you feel up to it, of course."

"I'd like that actually, I just feel...guilty, I suppose. I'm still so sad about the...baby, and I'm trying to keep a 'what was meant to be' mindset, and then there's this part of me trying to be happy about...whatever we are now, but in here..." She pressed her palm against her chest. "It still feels like an eruption could hit at any moment."

There had been less crying than yesterday, and Caz hoped it was a turning point, but Grace's eyes soon became watery again as she looked across the table at Caz.

"I think everything you're feeling is completely natural. And I also think...maybe we should tell people, a select few, but people like your mum and dad, Dani—they all think we're arguing and on the verge of divorce, especially after me having to get you from work and then neither of us leaving the house for days."

Grace smiled sadly. "If only they did know the truth... maybe we can tell them about the baby, I'm just not sure I can do it...or that I want to be there and have to deal with the fuss they'll make. You know what my mum's like."

"Lila loves you, and she has a strong opinion on how to show that sometimes—"

"She's too much at times like this...she'll want to take over and I know it's from a good place, but I don't think I have it in me right now to deal with that."

Caz snagged a slice of toast Grace had already buttered and bit into it as she said, "So I can tell them. I'll make it clear there's to be no big deal made of things and that you'll come to them when you're ready to talk about it."

She watched as Grace's bottom lip quivered and the tears that had been welling began to flow.

"I just feel like such a failure."

Caz moved quickly to be by her side, putting her arms around her. "No, that's not it at all." Her own tears appeared and she blinked rapidly to keep them at bay. "Sometimes, things aren't meant to be...maybe there's a different path for us."

"I hope so. This just feels so incredibly unfair."

"I know...and you know what?" She slapped her hands down on her thighs and stood up. "I'm going to book us a couple of days away. Let's just go somewhere and relax, get wrapped up in each other, and do whatever healing we need to do."

Grace wiped her face. "Really?"

"Yeah, your dad will be fine with it once he knows and I'm sure your boss is cool with you taking whatever time off you need, and if he isn't, well, tough…"

"Can we go…can you see if the beach house is free?"

"Are you a mind reader now, too?" Caz laughed. "That's exactly what I was going to look at first." She pulled her phone from her pocket, swiped the screen, and found the booking app. "It's almost October. I can't see there being much call for a beach house when the weather is like this…" She looked towards the window at the rain sliding down in sheets. "Here we go…" She scrolled down the page to the booking calendar. "Yes, it's free tonight through 'til Monday…"

"Let's do it—let's go now."

"Hold on." Caz pressed buttons and swiped, and typed, and pressed, and then smiled. "Okay, it's booked. You pack, I'll go and talk to your parents." She pressed a quick kiss to Grace's lips and then stopped. "If that's alright with you?"

"Anything you do…is alright with me," Grace said, and just for a moment, Caz felt sure that meant a lot more than speaking to Ron and Lila. "I won't be long."

"Okay. I'll pack for you too. Jeans, jumpers and shirts."

"Can't go wrong." Caz smiled and pushed herself back up to her feet. "I'll be back in a bit."

CHAPTER FORTY-SIX

Caz called ahead and asked Ron for a meeting, and for Lila to be there, which had garnered a multitude of questions, all of which she dodged with an, "I'll be there soon."

When she arrived, she noticed two things: Lila's Mercedes was parked in the corner, meaning she was already here, and Dani was finishing off a set of tyres and beckoning her over.

"What's up? You alright?" Dani asked, running a greasy hand over her head when Caz approached.

"Yep, but I need to talk to you—in private. Come up to Ron's office when you're done."

Dani nodded. "Sounds ominous. You ain't leaving, are you?"

"Nothing like that, but…it's important."

"Okay, I'll be right up. Just got to screw this back on." She pointed to the wheel and Caz walked away.

Waving a hand at some of the lads, Caz didn't stop for a chit-chat. Instead, she made her way up the stairs to Ron's office, striding up the steps like a woman on a mission. Because she was on one: A mission to make her wife's life better in any way she could, including dealing with her parents.

At the door, Caz paused. This was going to be tough—emotional. She could imagine Lila's response being much like Grace's, only more dramatic. She rubbed her face vigorously and blew out a breath. "You can do this," she said to herself, and then she knocked.

"Come in," Ron bellowed.

Opening the door, she could see him instantly, sitting in his chair like usual, at the desk with a steaming mug of tea to one side of his left hand.

Lila was perched on the other side, craning her neck over her shoulder to see who it was. When she realised it was Caz, she jumped down and straightened her skirt.

It was her who spoke first.

"Caz, whatever is going on?" She looked serious as she stood beside Ron, her left palm now resting on his shoulder.

"Grace and I—"

"Are you splitting up?" Lila asked, her back stiffening, "Where is Grace?"

"No, we're not, that's not why I asked you here," Caz was saying before another knock on the door came and Dani poked her head in. "Come in," Caz ordered and pulled the door open, closing it once Dani was inside.

Dani glanced around, uncertain, but didn't say anything.

Caz took a moment, resting one palm on the glass, the other on the door handle, and her forehead against the wood.

"Caz?" Ron said gently.

Slowly, Caz turned and looked around the room at the three quizzical, frowning faces. All the way over, she'd thought about what she'd say, but now, with them all looking at her and expecting answers, she felt a little dumbfounded.

"The thing is...Grace and I, we..." She felt tears threaten and blinked furiously to stop it. "Grace is..."

"Oh my God, they are, they're splitting up, Ron, I can't believe it, I can't. I thought this was it for our Gracie."

"We're *not* splitting up," Caz said more firmly than she'd intended. "We were having..." She closed her eyes and composed herself.

"It's alright, Caz, just say it," Dani encouraged.

"Grace has had a miscarriage," Caz said quietly and waited. When nobody else spoke, she continued, "This was our second attempt. The first didn't take, but this time...Grace was pregnant, and the other day—"

"What? Why didn't she tell us she was pregnant?" Lila asked, her flabber clearly ghasted.

"Because we were waiting for the three-month mark and...that didn't happen."

"Was that why you rushed out of here because Grace was unwell?" Ron asked.

"Kind of. It had happened over the weekend, but Grace needed to...she wanted to go to work and pretend like nothing had happened. That's why I was late. We were arguing over it. I wanted us to stay home and grieve, but she needed to be busy—"

"And now? Why isn't she here telling us this?" Lila stared at Caz like a lion guarding its cubs.

"Well, as you can imagine, she's pretty upset and she didn't feel as though she could talk about it with everyone yet, but...we decided it was only fair you knew what was going on, rather than assuming we're splitting up...which is really shitty by the way."

Lila looked full of shame and glanced to the floor, and then back at Caz. "Well, yes, I mean...I'm sorry, I shouldn't have said that."

"Is she alright? Really?" Ron asked gently.

"She's sad, Ron. Distraught, actually. We had a lot of plans and dreams about a future we might now not have so...she's working that out. We always knew it was a longshot, but we were hopeful. Grace is okay in herself, she's not depressed or suicidal if that's what you're worrying about."

"No, I didn't mean...well, maybe, I just...it's hard isn't it, not being able to speak to her."

"She's just overwhelmed at the minute. We're going to go away for a few days and I'm sure, at some point, she will feel up to talking with you."

Dani stepped forward. "And what about you?"

That was all it took.

Four words and the look of someone who truly cared asking, and Caz couldn't hold it in any longer.

"I'm devastated," she managed, before covering her face with her hands and sobbing. "For the baby, but mostly...for Grace."

Dani reached her first, and then Lila, both women guiding her to the sofa and sitting one either side, while Ron looked on. Unsure if he had anything wise to add, he kept quiet.

"It will be alright," Lila said. "These things happen."

"I know, I just wish I could make it different for Grace."

"That's because you love her and she loves you. And together, you'll get through this," Lila added.

"I do, I do love her, and she loves me, and we will get through this...I just...I need to get back to her." She stood up and ran her hands over her face, wiping away the tears and sadness.

Ron thrust his hand into his jacket pocket, pulled out his wallet and rifled through the notes, before pulling them all out. He got up and met Caz in the middle of the room. Pushing the notes into Caz's hand.

"I don't need—"

Ron held his hand up. "Whatever you both need, you only have to ask. Get her something nice. I don't care what you spend it on, just…take care of my Sweetpea. And take as much time as you need. Don't rush back to work. If Grace needs you at home, you stay at home, okay?"

Caz nodded. "Okay, thanks, Ron."

CHAPTER FORTY-SEVEN

"I'm home," Caz called out as she opened the door. Pulling her coat off, she kicked her shoes off and glanced into the lounge, finding it empty. "Grace?"

"I'm upstairs," came the response, and then Caz looked up to find Grace leaning over the banister. "Did it go okay?"

"Yeah." Caz nodded. She wouldn't be mentioning her own moment of falling apart. "They're just worried about you, that's all."

"I know, I just…I can't right now, you know? But I feel a bit better. I'm just trying to be logical and not emotional about it. For now, anyway."

"Of course. I'm going to make a cuppa and then I'll come up and help finish packing and then we can get on the—" The doorbell rang. "Who's that?" Caz said, more to herself. She took a look out of the small side window beside the door and sighed. The black Mercedes was on the drive.

"Who is it?" Grace whispered.

Moving to the bottom of the stairs, Caz answered, "It's your mum."

Grace's eyes widened. "I thought you told them to stay away. I don't…I can't…Caz."

"I did. It's okay, I'll deal with it. Stay up there."

Lila knocked with the letterbox, pushing it open to shout through the hole, "Grace?"

"For fuck's sake," Caz muttered before opening the door and forcing a smile. She stood with one hand on it as she stepped

213

into the small space, her other hand landing on the door frame, blocking Lila from entering. "Lila, I thought I just explained—"

Lila sagged. "I want to see my daughter, Caz."

"I know, and I've explained she doesn't want to see anyone."

"Caroline, step aside," Lila said, clearly more annoyed than she'd ever been with her daughter-in-law.

"I can't do that," Caz said, standing firm. "Like I said, Grace doesn't want to see anyone right now."

Lila threw her hands up dramatically. "I'm her mother," she shouted.

"And I'm her wife," Caz said, just the hint of irritation in her voice. "She has said she doesn't want visitors. So, until that changes, I'm sorry, but no. I will let you know when she's ready, or she will call, but I have to say, Lila, I'm very disappointed in you."

She closed the door and waited to make sure Lila didn't try again. When she heard the engine start up and the throaty sound of it roaring out of the driveway, she wandered down to the kitchen to make the tea she'd promised. Halfway through filling the kettle, she heard a small cough from behind and spun around to find Grace staring at her.

"What? Are you alright?" Caz asked.

The intensity of Grace's stare unnerved her—no—excited her. There was something there that she'd not seen directed at her before.

Grace continued to look at her, head tilting slightly to one side as her eyes narrowed.

"You just told my mother off and sent her packing."

Caz chewed her own bottom lip. "Yeah, that's what you wanted, right? Did you change your mind? I can call her—"

She didn't have time to finish the sentence before Grace crossed the room with all the gusto of someone on a mission. She grasped Caz's face between both palms and pulled her closer, pressing her lips to Caz's mouth. "That was..." she said between kisses, "the hottest thing..." Caz's hands slid around her waist. "I've ever witnessed you do."

The kiss intensified, past any level of heat they'd ever reached previously. Caz found herself pinned to the counter. Tongues battled in a duel for supremacy. Caz felt her fingertips moving, grasping at the material blocking them from touching the flesh she'd desired for so long.

"Grace..." Caz said when she finally had the sense to pull back. "What is happening?"

Getting her breath back, Grace covered her mouth with her hand, before lowering it and admitting, "I don't know, but I suddenly felt this surge of...I guess, attraction?"

When Grace then giggled, Caz felt torn. She wanted Grace to feel better, after all, and though laughter sounded good to hear, Caz felt it hit differently.

"Okay...and that's funny?"

"Yeah. I mean...you've always been protective of me. It was one thing when you told that bloke to back the fuck off, that was hot, but...my mum? That was...I'm sorry, I guess I just got lost in the moment and—"

Caz raised a brow as she stepped forward and pulled Grace closer again.

"So, what does this mean for...you know, us?"

"I guess maybe I can imagine us, like this...more... intimate..."

Caz nodded. "Noted. But to be clear, I am not taking advantage of your..."

"My mental state?" Grace smiled up at her.

"Exactly that." Caz leaned forward, kissing Grace gently. "In our own time, okay?"

CHAPTER FORTY-EIGHT

She couldn't get it out of her head. Despite her sadness over the baby, and their dreams for the future, Grace Hart-Madden, as she'd decided she wanted to be known from now on, had something to distract herself with: The kiss.

Not just the kiss, but the intensity with which she'd needed it—needed Caz. It had been more than nice. But there was a worry there, too. Was she using it just to distract her emotions away from the pain of losing the baby?

She chanced a side-eye glance at Caz and smiled.

No, she told herself, they were two separate issues.

She'd wanted to kiss Caz like that for a while; she could acknowledge it now. It turned her on and she could admit that too. She was noticing a lot about Caz lately; things she'd never allowed herself to really think about before.

How had she never seen it?

"It's good to see you smiling again," Caz said as she drove them towards the beach house.

Grace turned to her and sighed dreamily, reaching out her hand to place it easily on Caz's thigh, because that's what lovers did, didn't they?

"Yeah."

She noticed the way Caz casually glanced down at the move and she gave a little squeeze for good measure. She'd never done this before with Caz—something so intimate and casual—but it felt right. It felt...nice.

The weather had cleared a little—at the least the rain had stopped—and in the distance there were shades of blue peeking through the clouds.

"It's kind of like me," Grace said, now looking ahead.

"What is?" Caz indicated and overtook the slow-moving car in front.

"The sky...it's mostly grey, but...the sun's trying to come out, and brighter bits are peering out from behind the clouds." She turned her attention back to Caz. "I think that's how I feel... brighter bits are there, in the background, and slowly, they're making their way to the front."

Now Caz had finished her manoeuvre and pulled back into the slower lane, she let her hand land on top of Grace's, still on her thigh.

"That sounds really good."

"Can we go to that restaurant again? The one that overlooks the beach?"

"Absolutely. I've been dreaming about those burgers." Caz smiled quickly at her before putting her eyes back on the road.

Grace was quiet for a moment, looking out of the window at the fields whizzing by as she said, "Can we sleep naked together once this bleeding stops?"

"Uh, I guess we could," Caz said, a little unsure. "Won't you be cold?"

Grace turned to face her. "I don't think so. You'd keep me warm."

"I am hot stuff, that's true," Caz joked, before getting serious and asking, "Are you sure you want that?"

"Yes," Grace replied firmly. "We should be comfortable undressed around each other, don't you think? We've been living together for over a year now, we're married, and we—you know, we want to be more intimate with each other at some point, right?"

Caz nodded.

"I just think it might be a way of gently easing us there." Grace continued, "You know, so we get used to the idea of each other in that way..."

"I'm happy to go at any speed you feel is—"

"Maybe we should just have sex? Rip the Band-aid off, so to speak?"

"That wasn't... I mean, we could, but I didn't mean that... I don't think sex should ever be planned. It happens when it happens. I meant that... I'm happy to go along with whatever you need in order for you to feel more comfortable in any aspect of this...or not, if you change your mind and decide you don't—"

"I won't," Grace said firmly, again. "You're it for me, and I... I'm attracted to you. It's not that I don't want to be intimate...I guess, I'm just scared about it."

She could see Caz's mind working out how to answer that.

"I'm not scared of you, or us... Scared is the wrong word. I'm worried I won't know what I'm doing and you'll be disappointed, or I won't enjoy certain things and *I'll* be disappointed and then—"

"Grace?"

"Yes?"

"Do you like orgasms?" Caz asked as casually as if she were asking if Grace liked strawberries and cream.

"Of course I do."

Keeping her eyes on the road, Caz continued, "Okay, and when men have gone down on you, you liked it?"

Grace felt her cheeks burn but she answered Caz's

question, "Yes, I did...well, mostly...some were better than others."

Caz ignored that, preferring not to dwell too much on the men that had fumbled relationships with this beautiful creature in the past. On the other hand, she was grateful for that, too, because without them, they wouldn't be in this situation now. She stopped thinking about men who had nothing to do with their marriage and got her mind focused back on what she was trying to say.

"And when they did, did they look like it wasn't a pleasant experience?" She turned to face her. "And if you say yes, I want names and I'm going to go and punch them in the face for making you feel bad."

Grace laughed. "No, none of them looked like they didn't enjoy it."

Caz grinned. "Good...and did you reciprocate?"

"Yes."

"Even when it got messy and—"

Grace squeezed Caz's thigh hard. "Yes. Please don't ever say that out loud again."

Now it was Caz who laughed. "Okay, okay..." She cleared her throat. "So, what makes you think going down on me, or touching me intimately, or me doing that with you, will be something you won't like?"

Grace turned back to face forward and stare out of the window again. "You have a point."

"I know," Caz said, and indicated to get past the next slow driver to impede their journey. "So, sleeping naked? I can do that."

CHAPTER FORTY-NINE

Biting into the juicy beef burger, with its toasted bun and fresh lettuce, pickles, and whatever heaven was in that sauce, Caz groaned in appreciation.

"This is so good," she said between chews. "I might order another one."

Grace pinched a chip from Caz's plate and chomped it in two bites. Her own salad with grilled chicken was just as nice, but who didn't like chips?

"We can eat here every day if you'd like." Grace grinned at Caz and stole another chip. But then her attention moved to behind Caz and the sound of a baby mewling and crying in a pram, two tables away.

Caz put her burger down and wiped her hands before she reached across to Grace.

"Alright?" she asked.

Grace blinked away the tears and focused back on Caz as she tried to smile through her sadness.

"Yes. I guess it's going to take time, right?"

Caz nodded sympathetically. "Do you want to leave?"

Shaking her head, Grace picked up her fork and stabbed another chip. "Not until you've enjoyed every mouthful of that burger...and I've eaten your chips."

Caz pushed the bowl towards her. "I guess I can let you snag those bad boys, but...I will want something in return."

"Oh, and what would that be?"

Caz shrugged and picked up her burger again. "Might involve kissing me later."

"I didn't need bribing for that." Grace smiled and bit into another chip. It was nice, the way her eyes could just stare into Caz's and it didn't feel weird anymore. She could get lost in them and let herself imagine more.

"Well, look who we have here, Morgan." A familiar, friendly voice broke the spell between them as they both turned and looked up to find Alex grinning at them. "How are you both?"

"Hey," Caz said, standing to greet them. Grace still looked starstruck. "We're...yeah, we're good, I think?" She turned to Grace for confirmation that it was okay to tell them more.

Grace nodded.

"Yes, we..." Grace felt her cheeks blush. "Things have progressed."

"Wow, that's wonderful." Morgan clapped happily. "You should come over tonight and tell us all about it. If you don't have any other plans, of course."

"Yes, we're having an orgy," Alex said with a straight face. She couldn't hold it up, though, when three sets of eyes all widened and panic set in. "I'm kidding. It would be lovely to catch up." She touched Grace's shoulder as they moved past. "The sun sets on the deck around eight?" she called back to them.

"Sounds great." Caz held a thumb up. "You okay with that, really?" she asked Grace when they were out of earshot and she'd sat back down again. "We don't have to go if you just want to veg out—"

"No, I think it will be nice and...strangely, they're the only people who know everything about us...we can just be ourselves." She nabbed another chip. "And it will be a distraction, won't it?"

"Yes, so…"

"Let's just play everything by ear. If it comes up…we can tell them, that's okay, but I'll probably—"

"Cry? Yeah, that's what I thought. We don't have to say anything at all."

Grace smiled. "We can't pretend it hasn't happened,"

"I guess not, but equally, I don't want you feeling pressure to put on a happy face."

"I read a quote this morning that said, '*I am not sad, but sadness is on me.*' I'm not putting on a happy face. I'm genuinely happy with my life, with you, with us and the potential of what that means, and spending time with celebrities, drinking wine we could never afford." She picked up her napkin and wiped her lips. "And at the same time, I have sadness for what isn't meant to be. But life cannot stop. I have to keep going and find joy in things so this sadness lifts and doesn't burrow deeper. Does that make sense?"

"Perfect sense." Caz smiled and reached for her hand.

CHAPTER FIFTY

"What has it been—three, four months?" Alex asked as she handed out glasses—wine for three of them, beer for Caz.

"Something like that," Caz replied. "Thanks," she said, taking the glass.

"We've often talked about you both, wondering how you were getting on. Really, we should have swapped numbers, or email at least," Morgan said.

"Yes, it's not often one meets people who just...click, as they say." Alex smiled at Grace, who as yet, hadn't said much more than hello and a thank you.

"We should definitely do that, and you should both come and visit us when you're our way," Caz said, keeping the conversation light.

"Near Woodington, wasn't it?" Morgan asked. She looked well, but tired, and she stifled a yawn. "Sorry, long shift. I'm actually being considered for a job at Woodington Hospital."

"That would be great," Grace said, smiling at her. "We live in Banbury Hollow, kind of squeezed in between Woodington and Bath Street, but yes, like Caz said, you should visit. We'd love that."

"There's a great development by the river, near the meeting point of Banbury, Bath Street, Woodington, and Amberfield...that's the posher part." Caz laughed. "Lots of shops and restaurants, even a gay pub, and then there's the gay bar called Art, too, in Bath Street."

Morgan looked at Alex, pleading in her eyes. "Oh, we have to go. You've been promising me a night out for months."

Alex chuckled. "True. Maybe we will take you both up on that offer."

"So, how are you both?" Grace asked.

"The papers are bored of me, so that's been lovely." Alex smiled. "Of course, now I have nothing much to do, and Morgan is swamped at work...Sod's law, isn't it?"

"Well, if I get the job in Woodington, I'll have more time... A&E is great, but exhausting," Morgan admitted.

"They will be lost without you," Alex said, looking at her as though there was nobody else in the room with them.

Grinning, Morgan leaned over and kissed her—nothing too intense in itself, but the look they shared said so much more, and instinctively, Grace shuffled closer to Caz.

"Keep that thought for later," Alex whispered, but they all heard it. Not that she cared, as she turned to Grace and said, "So, what brings you to the beach in this weather?"

"We...just wanted to get away, and we had such a lovely time here before, it felt perfect," Grace answered, reaching for Caz's hand. The other women both caught the move and smiled at it. "Our relationship has maybe taken a turn towards something more...traditional—"

"Yeah, and we figured we'd get away for a bit and explore that somewhere neutral...but equally, somewhere that felt familiar too."

Morgan's eyes lit up. "Oh, this is so exciting. I said to Alex I thought you two were super cute together and it was absolutely clear you adored each other."

"And yet, you both look a little...sad?"

"We're still figuring it all out," Caz said, squeezing an arm around Grace and kissing the top of her head.

"I had a miscarriage recently," Grace said, surprising

herself as much as everyone else.

It was Morgan who reacted first. "I'm so sorry, Grace, and you too, Caz. You must be devastated, I'm sure."

"Yes, that is sad news," Alex added.

Caz lifted her bottle of beer from the table. "We're just taking our time with it, you know, it's all a bit raw."

Morgan and Alex nodded simultaneously.

"It happens more often that you'd think," Morgan offered. "If you ever need to talk about it..."

"Thank you. I might take you up on that," Grace said, "... once I'm ready...it feels like all I've done lately is talk."

Silence enveloped them all for a moment.

"I'm sorry, I've brought the mood down," Grace said, trying to smile. "I was telling Caz about a quote I read that said the sadness is on me, but I am not sad. That brings comfort." She took Caz's hand when it was offered. "And of course, it forced us to examine what we really are and what we both want."

"And that is something that is making us happy," Caz offered, now taking a sip from the bottle.

"Well, then, a toast," Alex said, raising her glass. "To love, and all the routes to it..."

"To love," they all chimed back as the glasses clinked together.

CHAPTER FIFTY-ONE

The walk back along the sand, and up the short street to the cottage, had taken longer than it had taken to stroll there, five hours earlier.

Several beers and glasses of wine meant a lot of stumbling and giggling as each of them swayed or wandered off course and added a few extra minutes to the journey.

Now, with Grace leaning against the door, Caz having one arm around her to hold her up while her other hand fiddled with the keys, it was almost three in the morning.

"Shh, you're going to wake everyone up," Grace warned, with just the hint of a slur to her words.

"*You* are everyone." Caz laughed and finally pushed the key into the lock. As it turned, the door opened and they both almost fell through it, causing another fit of giggles as Caz landed on the arm of the sofa, pulling Grace on top of her to save her from falling.

"Hi." Grace grinned, as she now hovered above Caz. "Do you prefer your women on top?"

"Sometimes," Caz flirted back, "if they can handle it."

"I can handle it," Grace said, leaning down to kiss Caz, "if you show me."

"What do you want me to show you?" Caz said, following it up with a hiccup and a wriggle as she tried to toe the door closed with her foot and failed.

Grace moved until she was straddling Caz's midriff. "Everything."

"You're drunk." Caz giggled.

"I am…" She pushed herself back up, palms resting against Caz's shoulders. Then Grace exhaled slowly and slid her hands lower until each one covered the softness of Caz's breasts. It was the first time she'd intentionally touched anywhere quite so intimate on the body of her best friend.

Their eyes locked, and for a moment the silence was palpable. Slowly, Caz moved her gaze away from Grace's face and let her eyes roam until they were fixed on palms that now kneaded gently.

"Is this…okay?" Grace asked. All of the alcohol-fuelled daring she'd started with seeming to dissipate into a nervous disposition.

"Yes," Caz answered with enough confidence for them both, as her right hand raised and slid behind Grace's neck, pulling her closer and back into a kiss that said more in its intensity than any drunken words might.

Caz's left hand landed against Grace's thigh—bare skin, warm to the touch from where her skirt had ridden up. Without thinking, her fingers caressed and inched higher until they cupped the silk-clad backside she'd been trying so hard not to think about all these weeks.

"Is this alright?"

"Yes," Grace whispered, moving in to continue kissing Caz.

From her supine position, Caz could only register two things: She loved kissing Grace, and it was freezing.

"Mmph, Grace, we should…" She didn't want to pull away. Neither did Grace with the way her lips were chasing Caz's, nipping and biting, encouraging them to return.

"Shh, just kiss me."

"Door…open…" Caz managed, before Grace thrust her

tongue back into Caz's mouth and she groaned and submitted to it until cold air became a sobering factor.

"Grace." She managed to extricate herself enough to create an inch of space between them.

Grace smiled at her, still a little drunk, but fully aware of what they were doing.

"Caroline..." she said with a little flirty wink.

"Don't you 'Caroline' me." Caz laughed, and wriggled until she could twist enough to drop Grace onto the couch and roll out, landing with a thump on the floor. "Door needs closing, and you need to get to bed..."

"Yes, with you."

When Caz turned around, she found Grace kneeling on the sofa with her top off. It was a sight she had seen dozens of times before and yet, now, right here, it felt new. She stared and understood how much she enjoyed a naked collarbone, the curve of shoulder into neck, and watching shoulder muscles strain when arms reached behind, deft fingers loosening the bra.

"Uh, as much as I would really...and I mean really, like this to go further...you are not in any state to make proper decisions." Caz slurred a little and swayed slightly before righting herself. "And neither am I..."

"Are you sure about that?" Grace mused, head tilting to the side as the flimsy material of her bra slid down her arms and revealed her breasts.

Caz closed her eyes and breathed deeply, uttering a silent prayer this moment would come again, before her eyes opened and locked onto Grace's and she said, "Yes. I'm sure."

Grace scrunched up her face. "Spoilsport."

"I know..." Caz moved closer, touching Grace's face tenderly. "And anyway, we can't touch..." She glanced downwards. "You're still bleeding and that's... I'm never going to be so drunk I put my needs before your wellbeing," she said, quickly followed by a hiccup.

"And that's why I love you," Grace whispered.

CHAPTER FIFTY-TWO

Forgetting to close the curtains the night before, Caz was woken by the stream of glorious sunshine that poured in through the window and rested on her face.

Bleary-eyed, she rolled away from it and into the back of Grace, who had already pulled the duvet up and over her head.

"Make it go away," she said when Caz pressed up against her.

Yanking the duvet higher, Caz joined her under it and kissed the bare shoulder, reminded instantly of the previous night and how it had ended with Grace half-naked, as she still was now. The skirt had fallen into a material-shaped puddle, and Grace had quickly visited the bathroom before hurrying back and climbing into bed to become a human limpet around Caz.

Not that Caz had minded at all. She'd slept in her underwear, too.

"Do you want to get up or go back to sleep?" Caz asked.

"Tired," Grace said, her hand shifting to move backwards and land on Caz's hip. "Go sleep."

Caz chuckled and tightened her hold on Grace. "Okay."

They drifted back to sleep for what felt like minutes, but had, in fact, been several hours, when Grace groaned and crunched up.

"Grace?"

"I'm okay, just cramps. They said I might get some as

everything settles."

"Do you need me to do anything?"

"No. If it continues, I'll take some painkillers. They shouldn't last more than a few days. The bleeding could stop at any point, too."

Grace turned to face Caz.

"Morning."

"Hey…" Grace looked tired and sleepy as her eyes battled to open fully. "What do you want to do today?"

Caz shrugged. "I don't mind. Happy to stay right here, or I can google for something to explore."

"Sounds nice, but first…coffee." She flung the cover to get up but was stopped by Caz holding her tight.

"I'll make you coffee—you rest."

Grace smiled, but said, "I'm not an invalid."

"Until you are one hundred percent again, you're going to rest and be waited on like a princess." She reached for her T-shirt that was on the end of the bed and pulled it on. "Which, let's face it, is like most days anyway," Caz joked, and wriggled away before Grace could pinch, poke, or tickle her in retribution.

But she wasn't quick enough and Grace grabbed her shirt, pulling her back towards her, and like lightning, Grace pinned her down and straddled her.

Staring down at Caz, her hair falling around her face, she said, "Do you want to pay now, or later when I've thought about your punishment a little longer?"

"Um…can I think about it?" Caz laughed, as fingers dug into her ribs and began to tickle. "Okay… Later?"

Grace eased up on her assault—a big mistake—because Caz took the opportunity to flip her off her body and over, and landed in the exact same position, now straddling Grace.

"Oh, would you look at that?" Caz teased. "Now, what could I possibly do next—"

Grace didn't hesitate. "Kiss me."

"That wouldn't be a punishment, would it?" Caz answered.

Easing up onto her elbows, Grace said, "You haven't brushed your teeth. I'd say that was punishment enough."

"Oh, now you're going to get it, lady." Caz laughed and began to tickle her. Grace wriggled and pleaded and laughed, and in that moment, Caz wondered if they might be okay again.

"Okay, you win." Grace laughed as she grabbed Caz's hands and tried to pry those strong fingers away from her ticklish ribs.

When Caz relented, Grace still held her hands. Lacing their fingers together, she let them fall to the pillow, making Caz hover above her.

"You know, we should have a conversation."

Caz cocked her head. "Oh, about what, exactly?"

"Sex."

Still holding her hands and pressing them into the soft pillow, Caz rose up slightly. "I thought we'd talked about that in the car."

"I mean, we began the discussion..." Grace smiled up at her. "How will we know if we're even compatible?"

"How do you mean?"

"Well." Grace tried to sit up, but Caz held her firmly down. "This, for instance..." She stared into Caz's eyes. "Holding me down, is that something you like doing?"

Caz went to release her but was stopped when Grace gripped harder.

"No, don't do that." Grace shook her head. "Answer the question..."

Licking her lips, Caz looked away for a moment. "I like it if you like it."

"Oh...okay, that wasn't what..." This time, Grace let go and did sit up, her pretty face frowning. "For reference, I do like it, but...what do you mean you like it if I like it?"

Caz began to fidget, uncomfortable with the question.

"Caroline Iris Madden—"

"Okay, don't go down the whole full name route..." Caz said, taking a breath and exhaling. "I'm just...I guess I'm pretty simple in bed. I don't have...I'm not into...what I like is more about mental stimulation and being wanted and then, the basics. I don't have fantasies—I'm not kinky."

Grace touched her cheek. "Why is this making you emotional?"

"I don't know. I just feel...embarrassed, I guess. Women get to know me, and they take my confidence as a sign that I'm into something funky."

"And you're not?"

"Not consciously," she answered. "I think I just go with whatever feels right, you know? Like...I don't have any set idea on what will turn me on...or off. Sometimes I can be somewhat dominant, but then other times I can be led...but I'm not a switch."

"A switch?"

"Yeah, so there are tops, bottoms, and switches...I'm a top in that respect."

Grace frowned. "You're going to have to explain that for me. You're not dominant, but you're a top?"

"Yeah…so, a top does the…penetrating. They don't want to be on the receiving end of that, whereas a bottom does…and a switch is someone who likes both."

"So, you're a top…which is good, because I'd completely be a bottom, then." Grace smiled at her. "But you can switch between Dom/sub?"

Caz shrugged. "I guess so, yeah. It's only what I've read or heard people talk about."

Grace thought about it for a moment. "I like these descriptions. They make sense. I think I'm the same. There are times I like to be on top…in the straight sense of the word, literally on top of…well, you know." She chuckled. "Which leads me to my next question, then…do you use…toys?"

"Yeah, if you—"

"If I want to…" Grace smiled as she finished the sentence. "Do you like it when someone you're sleeping with wants to?"

"What I like is…seeing, hearing, feeling her enjoying it. That's what I get off on."

Grace wriggled closer. "So, you're all about the senses?"

"I suppose so, yes." Caz smiled. "I've never thought about it like that before…I just thought…" She shrugged. "…thought I was a bit weird."

"I think you're special." Grace smiled at her. "I can't believe we've never talked about this before."

"Why would we?"

Grace shrugged. "I guess because I tell you everything, but I've just realised, the only time I've talked about relationships with you, is either when I just met them, or when it was over. We never shared details."

"Not sure I'd have been much use for het advice." Caz blushed, and took Grace's hand. "What about you then? What do you like?"

"Hm, hard to answer when my only experience is with men. I guess with them I liked it," Grace pressed her lips together before admitting, "...I kind of liked it rough...I liked it when you held my hands down and hovered above me just now. And it made me consider what that would be like if you were inside me."

"Okay...well, thanks for the heads up...I can definitely make that little fantasy come true." Caz winked.

"And I can be very...very...noisy about it when you do," she smirked, "but..." Grace held a finger up, "I also want to experience romance with you...I want you to love me, in every way you want to."

"Noted."

CHAPTER FIFTY-THREE

One foot in front of the other. That was all either Caz or Grace could think about as the rain lashed down on them and they concentrated on not losing their footing on the slippery mud-like path.

A walk across the South Downs had been the plan for their last full day at the beach before they headed back the next morning.

The sun was out, it was only a short car ride away, and the fresh air would do them both good. That was how Caz had sold it once they'd gotten up, dressed, and had had breakfast. That was until the weather decided otherwise and dark clouds had moved in at the mid-way point.

"Not what I had in mind," Caz moaned as they trudged back along the muddy path towards the car, the backside of her jeans covered in muck from where she'd slipped coming down a short slope.

"We're almost back at the car...though, you are not sitting on my leather seats with all that mud on you," Grace said, still giggling from the memory of Caz's slide.

"What am I supposed to sit on?" Caz held her palms out. "Do we have a blanket?"

Grace shrugged. "Nope, just take them off."

"I am not driving back in my pants," Caz said, incredulous. "Imagine if we get pulled over. Then what?"

"The police will have a good giggle?" Grace grinned.

"There has to be something I can sit on, or I'll just clean the seat when we get back," she said, until she noticed Grace staring at her, non-plussed. "Or I can just take them off."

"Do you see how much simpler it is when you do as you're told?" Grace continued to grin.

The car was in sight and Caz upped her pace, digging into her pocket for the keys.

"I've always done as I'm told, or have you never noticed the power you have over me?" Caz grabbed Grace's hand. "Come on, I'm hungry and I need a shower to warm up, and you...can join me."

From the car, Caz had headed straight in and stripped out of the rest of her clothes to quickly stand herself under the hot water of the shower.

With her face looking up, water cascading over her, she smiled when she heard the door creak open.

"Are you coming in?" she asked without opening her eyes, but when Grace didn't speak, Caz glanced back over her shoulder.

Grace was standing in the doorway, towel wrapped around her, hair brushed and hanging wet down her back. Her bottom lip was tugged between her teeth as she stared at Caz's bare backside.

"Caz?"

"Yeah?

Not wanting to put any pressure on Grace, Caz continued showering. Pouring shampoo into her palm, she reached up and began to massage the soap into her hair.

"I..."

Caz rinsed her hair and then turned to face Grace, watching as Grace looked at her for the first time, as her wife should look at her naked form.

"We don't have to—" Caz found her words dry up when Grace dropped the towel she'd been clutching around herself. "Or you could...do that." Caz smiled and held out her hand.

Grace took it and then took the first steps towards Caz.

"I never realised how...fit you are." Grace laughed. "I've seen you half-undressed loads of times and yet, I've never really looked at you, I suppose. You've got abs."

"You've got boobs." Caz grinned at her as Grace looked down at herself as though checking that were true. "You can touch me...if you want to."

For a moment, neither of them made a move, eyes furtively darting up and down each other as they tried to take it all in.

And just when Caz thought it all might be too much for her, Grace reached up, sliding her hand over Caz's shoulder and around her neck, stepping in close enough their bodies squished against one another, naked, skin-against-skin for the first time. "I want your mouth on me," she whispered against Caz's ear as she leaned in closer, "and your hands...I want to feel you touch me the way you want to...don't think about it, just touch me..."

Caz nodded, her palms lifting to rest against Grace's hips, soapy fingers gripping her flesh and pulling her closer. "We can't do—"

"We can...it's okay, I'm okay...you won't hurt me."

"I'd never hurt you."

Grace smiled. "I know, I was just making sure *you* know you won't..."

With warm water cascading down, Caz stopped thinking

and acted. The kiss was slow and tender and easy. It made perfect sense. Lips slid against one another, teasing and tantalising like they'd been doing a lot lately, only this time, they were both naked.

They twisted beneath the deluge until Grace had her back against the cool tiles, her leg raised and hooked around Caz's thigh.

It was somewhat erotic, at least, in Caz's mind. Before now, she hadn't dared to really imagine making love with Grace. Little snippets of sexy thoughts had seeped into her imagination at times, but never making love; never allowing herself to feel these emotions that were orchestrating her every move right now.

She took the lead, guiding Grace gently, instigating and initiating. Every moan or hiss of delight spurred her on to explore further and she ran her palms over stiff nipples and soft flesh, then rounded hips and buttocks, mapping everything in her mind while trying to concentrate and focus whenever Grace reciprocated.

It was their first time together and she wanted to remember every detail. *Their first time together,* repeated in her head. *Their first time together.*

She pulled back, breaking the kiss and catching her breath as she watched Grace's chest heave and her face frown.

"What's wrong...why are you stopping?" Grace asked, her voice carrying a little hint of insecurity.

Caz smiled, stroking her cheek. "I'm not...I'm just...I don't want our first time together to be standing in a shower when we have a perfectly sound bed to frolic in."

"Frolic?" Grace laughed and kissed her again. "God, I love you so much." She turned around and switched off the shower. "Lead the way to said frolicking."

CHAPTER FIFTY-FOUR

A sudden thought occurred to Caz as Grace pulled her into the bedroom.

"Are you still—"

Grace turned and shook her head. "No, it stopped."

"Not that it would really matter—there are ways around that..." Caz looked away before smiling awkwardly.

"Caz?"

"Yeah?"

"Stop talking." Grace grinned and pulled her closer. "We're both grown-ups, we're married, and we love each other...and we have a bed...so..." Her palms raised up and pushed against Caz's chest. Unprepared, Caz lost her balance and fell backwards onto the mattress, landing with her elbows supporting her weight. Grace immediately sat across her thighs and leaned forward. "I want this...with you."

It was an image Caz would burn into her memory banks. Dark hair fell around them both. She let her eyes explore the curves and arousal of the woman she loved more than any other person on the planet as she hovered above her.

One in eight billion.

How was it possible to find your match in a world full of potential? But she had.

She reached up, her palm gently caressing Grace's cheek. "Are you sure you want to do this now? We don't have to rush this."

"I think..." Grace leaned closer, "we've waited long enough, don't you?" She moved in, lips ready to press firmly against Caz's, when she stopped. "Unless...it's you that wants to wait?"

Caz shook her head. "No, I'm ready for this. For us." She craned her neck forward and met eager, waiting lips, her palm sliding further into Grace's hair, urging her closer until she all but lay flat against Caz.

As the kiss grew more intense, Caz used her strength to slowly turn them both until they'd switched places and she was on top, legs sliding either side of Grace's thigh.

It didn't take much before Grace moved and made more room, Caz's leg pressing harder until she was met with the arousal and firmness of Grace's bareness.

She smiled to herself as the first soft moan escaped Grace, a sound that instantly hit home with her own excitement.

She wanted more of it.

Her lips kissed a path along Grace's jawline, down her neck, and lower still, until she was face to face with that delicious collarbone.

"Do that again," Grace demanded, and Caz was only too keen to oblige, moving her thigh rhythmically, pressing more firmly when Grace bent her knees and pressed her heels into Caz's buttocks.

"Yes..." Grace nodded, more to herself, Caz considered, too focused on lavishing every inch of skin with kisses. So lost in it all, she barely felt it when Grace took her hand and pushed it lower. "Touch me, I need you to..."

Caz pushed herself up onto one elbow, looking down into those brown eyes she'd loved all these years.

"Touch...me," Grace almost begged.

"Show me how," Caz responded, now moving Grace's hand into the space between them. "Show me what you like…"

"Fuck, that's…nobody has ever asked that," she said between breaths, as her fingertips touched her clit and Caz slid her own hand on top.

"I want to know everything." Caz smiled down at her.

Caz focused on the movements, and the speed and pressure, enjoying the jerks and moans as Grace expertly got herself off.

When Grace pulled her hand free, Caz's remained, sliding her fingers lower and into the wetness, watching Grace's face as she inched inside of her for the first time.

They both took a moment to recognise it, to mutually understand they were now one, completely and utterly joined together in a way more intimate than either had ever known with anyone else.

Grace smiled. "Don't think about it, I won't break."

"How did you know I was thinking that."

"Because I know you, and I know you love me…and now…" She slid her hand around Caz's neck and pulled her face closer. "I want you to fuck me like you've never fucked anyone before."

"I want to hear you being fucked like you've never been fucked before," Caz said, her movements slow and teasing.

"Mm, so good," Grace purred, her back arching like a cat, and her grip around Caz's neck, grasping firmly, until her mouth was right next to Caz's ear and all Caz could hear were the soft moans that grew into incoherent words when she upped her speed and followed the instructions she'd been given.

She'd lost count at five.

"Okay…enough…I can't take…oh, fuck."

Grace groaned as the final swipe of Caz's tongue lashed against her clit and another eruption burst forth form her.

"Jesus, is this normally…" Her chest heaved, fingertips clutching at the sheet, as her hips jerked upward once more and she cried out one last euphoric ensemble of incoherent noise.

"So…much?" she finally stammered out.

Her legs clamped tightly around Caz, stopping any further pleasurable assault on that one spot Caz had discovered hours ago. Grace was sure it was hours, as she'd lost all track of time, and what was up and what was down.

When she finally relaxed and Caz was free to scuttle up the bed and kiss her, she could barely breathe, and then she burst into tears.

"Oh, that's not good…Grace?" Caz said, rolling onto her side and pulling Grace with her. "What's wrong?"

"Nothing…I'm fine." She tried to laugh through the tears. "Overwhelmed, I guess, that's all." She pulled Caz close, again attaching herself like a limpet, legs and arms wrapped tightly as her body shuddered and shook until it was finally spent.

"Okay?" Caz asked.

"Okay? Are you for real?" Grace laughed, and then she grew serious. "How am I supposed to live up to that?"

Caz grinned. "Practice, babe, lots of practice."

"What if—"

"Uh-uh." Caz pressed a finger to her lip. "It's not a

competition."

"Really?" Grace snapped her teeth at the finger. "I think it might become one...once I've practiced enough." She took Caz by surprise and flipped her onto her back. "So, I think we'll start here..." She leaned lower and sucked a nipple between her lips, enjoying the way Caz hissed her own pleasure, and then she trailed fingertips down the bare torso of her new lover. "Here..." She leaned back up and hovered above Caz. "I might have been the last to know...but I'm going to make up for every lost moment."

"And I'm here for it...'til death do us part."

FOR MORE INFORMATION

Claire Highton-Stevenson has written over thirty sapphic romance novels, including the Goldie award-winning, The Promise and the highly acclaimed, Scarlett Fever.

You can find Claire on almost all Social media platforms:

Facebook.
Instagram.
Patreon (Free).
YouTube.

For news about future books, podcasts, events etc, you can sign up to Claire's newsletter by visiting her website, www.itsclastevofficial.co.uk

Made in the USA
Columbia, SC
17 June 2025